A Captive in Rome

by Kathy Lee

© Kathy Lee 2005
First published 2005
ISBN 1 84427 088 2

Scripture Union, 207–209 Queensway, Bletchley, Milton Keynes, MK2
2EB, United Kingdom
Email: info@scriptureunion.org.uk
Website: www.scriptureunion.org.uk

Scripture Union Australia, Locked Bag 2, Central Coast Business Centre,
NSW 2252, Australia
Website: www.scriptureunion.org.au

Scripture Union USA, PO Box 987, Valley Forge, PA 19482, USA
Website: www.scriptureunion.org

British Library Cataloguing-in-Data
A catalogue record of this book is available from the British Library.

Printed and bound in Great Britain by Creative Print and Design (Wales),
Ebbw Vale

Internal illustration by Christopher Rothero
Cover design by GoBallistic
Internal design and layout by Author & Publisher Services

Scripture Union is an international Christian charity working with
churches in more than 130 countries, providing resources to bring the
good news of Jesus Christ to children, young people and families and to
encourage them to develop spiritually through the Bible and prayer.

As well as our network of volunteers, staff and associates who run
holidays church-based events and school Christian groups, we produce
a wide range of publications and support those who use our resources
through training programmes.

CONTENTS

1   The Battlefield 5

2   Survivors .12

3   Captured 17

4   The Slave Market 24

5   Sold 32

6   The Master's House 38

7   A Way of Escape 46

8   Beware of the Dog 52

9   Saturnalia 58

10 Finding Gold 66

11 Lessons 72

12 In the Arena 78

13 Life or Death 86

14 The Best Price 93

15 Freedom 100

16 Plans 108

17 No Goodbye 114

18 No Hope 121

19 Too Costly 129

20 Choices 136

To Rhona with thanks for all your help and advice

I

THE BATTLEFIELD

It was the day of the great battle. Long before sunrise, I was awakened by the noise and bustle in the camp. Excited voices, the neighing of chariot horses, the scrape of blades being sharpened...

I scrambled out from my sleeping place on the ground under our cart. My father and brother were up already. They had stripped off most of their clothes, shivering in the chill morning air, and were smearing each other with blue warpaint. It made them look wild and ferocious, changing them from ordinary people into bloodthirsty warriors.

Oh, why wasn't I allowed to join them? Conan was just 15, but he was counted as a man and a fighter. I was 11 — too young. I could only stand and watch, along with my mother and sisters.

Conan guessed how I felt. "At least you'll see everything," he said, trying to cheer me up. "You can tell your grandchildren you saw the last great battle, when we got rid of the Romans for ever."

"But *you* can tell your grandchildren you actually fought in it," I said enviously.

"What if I get myself killed? Then there won't be any grandchildren to tell."

But he was only joking. He didn't seriously think he would come to much harm. After all, we had ten times more fighters than the Romans had. How could we possibly lose?

Everyone wanted to see this great victory. That was why so many men had brought their wives and children along with them — normally we would have had to stay at home. I thought of the Romans in their camp on the hilltop. They would be getting ready too. They were trained soldiers, with armour, helmets and heavy shields. But armour hadn't saved the Romans in cities like Londinium. Our army had captured the city and burned it to the ground.

The Romans were probably praying to their gods, but that wouldn't save them either. Our gods were more powerful than theirs, and the Druids had made offerings so that our warriors would be protected.

The scarlet edge of the sun rose above the treetops. It was angry looking, like a blood-filled wound in the sky.

Looking up at it, I hoped we would see plenty of blood before nightfall — Roman blood. Then we would be rid of the enemies who had conquered our land. No more taxes to pay. No more fear. No more hiding of swords in haystacks and grain jars. (The Romans thought they had confiscated all our weapons, but they were wrong.)

I picked up Father's sword and looked at it longingly. I tried to imagine how I would feel if I could carry it into battle.

"Hey, Bryn! Put that down!" said Conan.

Father put his hand on my shoulder. "Your turn to fight will come soon enough," he said. "Don't run to meet trouble before it arrives."

***

My little sisters, Enid and Bronwen, were awake by now. I climbed onto the cart beside Enid, who was staring all around at the men in their battle gear.

"Look! That's Queen Boudicca," I said to her.

"Where? Where?" She craned her neck.

All around us a great cheer went up, and men waved their swords in the air. Out beyond the shouting warriors, the queen's chariot raced across the open hillside. The charioteer reined in the horses, and the queen stood up tall and proud, her red hair streaming in the wind.

"Now she'll make a speech," I told Enid. We were too far back to hear her words, but we could see how fiercely she waved her spear. It was easy to guess what she was saying. Death! Death to all Romans! Freedom for the Celtic tribes!

And the different tribes for once stood together like one nation, forgetting their old quarrels. They yelled their battle cries. Death to all Romans!

Suddenly, above the shouting, I heard another sound — the blast of a trumpet. On the hilltop, the sun glinted on metal. The Romans were on the march.

Many times I had seen Roman soldiers marching. They were all identical, wearing the same uniform, keeping the same pace — left, right, left, right. Orders were given and they obeyed, as if they couldn't think for themselves. They would march for miles on the long, straight roads they had built across our land. Left, right, left, right.

The Romans took up their positions in rows near the top of the hill, where thick woods protected them on each side. The front line of soldiers lifted their shields to form a wall, and the rows behind held their shields above their heads like a roof. It was quite impressive, I had to admit. All you could see were shields and legs.

Enid laughed. "They look like a giant centipede."

"Yes, and we'll stamp on them and squash them like centipedes," I said, scornfully.

Our army had no trumpet giving orders. That wasn't the Celtic way of fighting. When the queen's chariot turned towards the enemy, a wild shout went up, and all the warriors surged forward, eager for the glory of the fight.

In the lead were the chariots — not as swift as usual, for the hill was steep. Then came the great mass of swordsmen on foot. They had no heavy armour to weigh them down. Some had small, round shields, but their main protection was their courage and skill with the sword.

I would have given anything to join them. I didn't have a sword, just my knife. But that was sharp enough to slit open a fish... or a Roman.

"Bryn! Stay where you are," my mother told me. "I'm not having all my menfolk getting killed." Her face was white and anxious.

"Don't worry," I said to her. "We're going to win this easily. Nobody's going to get killed."

"There never yet was a battle where nobody got killed," she said, and I could tell she didn't want to be here. She thought we should have stayed safely at home, missing all the glory of the fight.

Our chariots had almost reached the Roman lines when the trumpet blared again. Hundreds of javelins came hurtling out from behind the shield wall. At that range, they couldn't miss. Horses screamed and reared up; drivers fell wounded; chariots collided at speed. I could hardly bear to look.

But now our swordsmen hurled themselves against the Roman shields, like a great wave thundering against a rock. Here and there, the Roman line appeared to break. Not for long, though. Men from the rows behind stepped forward to fill the gaps.

"The Romans are good fighters," Bronwen said, nervously.

"Yes, but we have a far bigger army," I told her. "We'll wear them down in the end."

The trouble was, the Roman leader had chosen the battlefield carefully. Because of the thick forests on either side, our army couldn't encircle his. We could only attack from in front, up the hill. Half our men couldn't even get near the enemy.

"Where's Father?" asked Enid. Even on tiptoe, she couldn't see very far. I was taller, but in that heaving mass of fighters it was impossible to make out anyone I knew. "Is he all right?"

I tried to tell her that Father would be safe, but the words seemed to stick in my throat. For I was seeing what a battlefield was really like. It wasn't like the songs of the bards, full of brave deeds and mighty heroes. It was just a confused mess.

Terrible sounds filled the air. Swords clashing, drums rattling, war horns blowing — those were the noises I'd expected to hear, but they were drowned by the cries of wounded men. People fell and were trampled underfoot. Horses screamed in agony.

Where was Father? And Conan, and the others from our village?

Once more, the trumpet sounded — and Roman horsemen came charging out of the woods to right and left. They took our army completely by surprise. Now our men had to fight on three sides. Slowly they gave ground, and the battle began to move downhill towards our camp.

Enid, looking scared, scrambled down from the cart. My mother grabbed Bronwen.

"Bryn, get down," she ordered me. "It's not safe here."

I shook my head stubbornly.

"I'm telling you — get down. We're getting out of here," she said.

"No! We can't leave now! I have to see what happens."

I suppose she knew she could never persuade me. She didn't waste time trying, but gathered up my sisters and hurried off through the camp. I hardly noticed them go. My eyes were fixed on the battlefield.

Things were going badly for us. That long line of Romans was on the move down the hill, pushing our men backwards. And there was nowhere for them to go. Their path was blocked by dozens of carts and wagons on the edge of our camp.

How could this be happening? We were being herded like sheep!

Our men at the front were still fighting fiercely, but they couldn't hold back that steady, merciless advance. At the rear, people were being crushed in the crowd. They escaped through the gaps between the wagons, or even crawled underneath them — but not fast enough.

Like a millstone pressing down on grain, the Romans pressed closer. I felt the cart move beneath me, then tilt and tip up. I was knocked to the ground, under the trampling feet of an army on the run.

Two or three times I tried to get up, struggling and shouting. Each time I was knocked down again.

Then something must have hit me on the head, for everything went black. That's all I remember.

II

SURVIVORS

"Bryn. Bryn! Wake up!"

Someone was shaking me. The shaking sent waves of pain through my skull.

"Oh, Bryn, come on! They'll kill us if we stay here!"

I struggled to open my eyes. My brother's face was close to mine. His warpaint was smudged and streaked. His eyes were red, as if he'd been crying.

Conan crying? Suddenly, I remembered. The battle — the Romans...

With a great effort, I managed to sit up. "Where's Father?"

Conan didn't answer. He looked up the hill, where dead and dying men lay like fallen leaves... hundreds of them, too many to count.

The fighting had moved on. There were no enemies in sight: no living ones, that is. Faintly in the distance, I heard the sound of a Roman trumpet.

"Where's Father?" I asked again. "Is he wounded?"
Still Conan said nothing.

"Is he dead?" I whispered.

"Yes. He's dead. And we'll die too if we're still here when the Romans come back."

"No!" I couldn't believe it. He couldn't be dead — not my father, so tall and strong!

"He died a warrior's death," said Conan. "He took three Romans with him. Look, I have his belt and his sword, and one day... one day I'm going to get revenge on the Romans for this." His voice trembled.

When I saw the sword, I knew it must be true — Father was dead. I would never see him again. I would never walk beside him, learning his skill at hunting and farming and fighting, never hear that laugh of his which seemed to shake the house.

He was gone, gone for ever. I felt as if a great storm had blown away the roof of our home. We were left huddled in the ruins, with nothing to protect us from the raging wind and the rain. Who would look after us now?

"Bryn, we have to be strong," said Conan. "We have to take care of Mother and the girls. Where are they?"

"I don't know. They went off through the camp — that way."

A trail of destruction led through the camp. There were more dead, this time women and children as well as warriors. The Romans seemed to have slaughtered anything that moved.

I felt sick. Would Mother, Bronwen and Enid be lying somewhere among the dead?

We began to search, but soon gave up. "This is hopeless," said Conan. "If they're here, we'll never find them."

"Maybe they got away," I said. "Maybe they ran off into the woods."

"That's what we should do — get away from here as fast as we can."

But first Conan began digging around in the wreckage of our cart. He found some clothes, a loaf and some dried meat. As he got dressed, fumbling awkwardly with the fastening of his cloak, I realised he was hurt. He had a deep gash across the back of his sword hand, with blood still oozing from it. I wanted to bandage it, but he wouldn't let me.

"There isn't time. The Romans will come back to their camp before nightfall."

He hurried me into the woods. We would be safer in the deep forest, even if there were wolves there. Better to meet wolves than Romans.

I kept looking around, hoping to see the rest of our family. But there was no sign of them. We saw a few people slipping between the trees. Here and there lay wounded men who had escaped from the battlefield but could go no further. There was nothing we could do for them, so we hurried on.

At last, exhausted, we stopped to rest and eat something. We were on a hilltop where the trees were thin. The forest stretched out below us, with cleared areas where villages stood among fields. In the distance, we could see the long, straight line of a Roman road.

"If Mother and the girls did get away," I said, "where would they go?"

"I think they would try to go home. But it might take days for them to get there."

"So we should go home too?"

He nodded. "If we can find the way," he said, looking uncertain.

I had always looked up to Conan. He was four years older than me and better at everything — fighting, running, hunting, storytelling. But now I saw that he was still not much more than a boy. He wasn't old enough to make decisions. Father always used to do that.

"Can't we just go back the way we came?" I asked.

"What, along the Roman road? Don't be stupid!"

Our home village lay to the south-east, only a day's journey away — if we used the Roman road. But we didn't want to meet any soldiers, not with Conan still in his warpaint. He had washed off as much as he could with water from a stream, but his face was still a pale bluish colour.

Our only hope was to go cross-country, taking our direction from the sun. All that afternoon and into the evening, we walked and walked. Soon we would have to stop, for the sun was going down, making long shadows between the trees. And at night the forest was not a good place to be. Wolves hunted there, and nameless fears lurked in the darkness.

I was glad when we came to a clearing. Across the fields we could see a village very much like our own — a huddle of round houses with roofs of thatch. If the people belonged to our tribe, the Iceni, they would shelter us for the night.

But there was something odd about the place. As we got closer, it was eerily quiet. No dogs barked at us. No children played around the doors. No cows mooed as they were brought in for milking. No smoke drifted up from the rooftops into the evening sky.

Conan lifted the curtain at the nearest doorway. I don't know what I thought we might find — more dead people, murdered by the Romans? But the place was empty.

"They must have heard that we lost the battle," said Conan. "They've all run away."

We looked at each other. Would we be safe here? But neither of us felt like spending the night in the forest. In the end, we decided to stay where we were.

Weary as dogs after a long day's hunting, we lay down on the straw bedding of the hut. But for a long time I couldn't sleep. I couldn't stop the memories of the day going round and round in my head. I kept thinking of my family.

When I fell asleep at last, I dreamed that everything was all right again. The battle had been won, not lost, and my father was still alive. The whole family was safe at home, with a great feast about to begin.

Then I woke up to a strange house and a cold hearth — and the pain of knowing that I would never see my father again, except in dreams.

III

CAPTURED

All the next day, thick, grey clouds filled the sky. Without the sun to guide us, we couldn't find our way through the forest — we might end up walking round in circles. So we stayed on in the empty village.

The owners had taken their most valuable belongings, their sheep and cattle. A few hens had been left behind to peck and scratch around the village. We hunted for eggs, which had to be eaten raw, as it would be too risky to light the fire. We also found a big pot half full of cold stew, so we didn't go hungry. But it was a long, silent, miserable day.

The open wound on Conan's hand was looking ugly. He kept brushing flies away from it. Mother would have put salve on it to help it heal, but Mother wasn't here. I washed it and bound it up with rough strips of cloth cut from the edge of a blanket.

I couldn't forget the sight of all those women and children, butchered by the Romans. If only I knew what had happened to my family!

"Do you think they managed to get away?" I asked.

"We just have to hope they did." But Conan didn't sound hopeful.

"They might be nearly home by now." I tried to imagine them on the path to our village, Mother walking slowly because she was carrying Bronwen, and Enid walking even slower on tired little legs.

"Will you stop going on about them!" Conan burst out angrily. "Just shut up. Talking won't help them. If they're dead, talking won't bring them back."

"But they may be all right. The gods may be on their side."

"The gods! They were supposed to protect us — that's what the Druids said. But they didn't. Our gods are powerless compared to the Roman ones."

"Shh," I said. "Don't talk like that. They'll hear you."

"I don't care if they do. They can't punish me, because they're useless. Useless, do you hear?" He cupped his hands and shouted across the valley, towards the encircling woods: "Useless!"

A faint mocking echo came back, and I gasped: "See! They heard you!"

Conan laughed. So did the echo.

Feeling nervous, for it's foolish to taunt the gods, I went back indoors. But there was no comfort to be found there. Night was falling. The hut, with no fire in the hearth, was like a dark cave, not a home. I felt a shiver run through me. What would we do if we reached our home village and found it as empty as this place?

And how would we survive through the next winter? Hardly any crops had been planted that spring because the men were all away at the war. With no grain stored up, and no men left to go hunting, it would be a hungry winter.

Everything had gone wrong. The future was dark and frightening. Maybe Conan was right — our gods were losing their power to help us. The Roman gods had invaded our land and conquered it, just as the Roman soldiers had conquered our people. But what could we do? You can't fight against the gods.

We went to bed as soon as it got dark. I lay still, listening to the sounds of the night — an owl hooting far away, a mouse rustling through the straw — and gradually drifted off to sleep. Suddenly, I was awoken by another sound, and fear gripped me by the throat.

Conan sat bolt upright. The same sound had awoken him too — the tramp of marching feet. The footsteps stopped, and a voice barked out an order in a foreign language.

Romans! Roman soldiers, right outside the door!

I looked around desperately. There was no place to hide, unless we burrowed into the straw. But no one came in. What was happening?

Then we smelled smoke, and heard the crackle and hiss of burning thatch. The Romans were burning the village, as our warriors had burned Londinium.

A bright flame flickered in the darkness above us. Sparks dropped onto the straw, setting it alight. If we didn't get out, we would burn to death! We ran towards the door.

"Stay in the shadows," Conan told me. "Head towards the trees."

But there were no shadows. All around us, the huts were ablaze like a ring of bonfires. As we ran out, a shout went up. Conan tried to pull Father's sword from its sheath. Too late — we were surrounded by soldiers. Although we both struggled fiercely, the soldiers quickly overpowered us. Conan wouldn't stop shouting angrily at the soldiers who seized us. I was sure we were about to die.

Then the leader gave an order. Instead of killing us, they took our weapons away and tied our hands. I felt my face burn with shame and fury.

It would be better to be killed than taken prisoner. That's what Father always said. Choose a warrior's death, not a lifetime of slavery!

But we had no choice. They led us away into the darkness.

***

"Where are they taking us?"

For three days, we had been marching southwards. We were part of a long, straggling line of prisoners, chained together in groups of five, with iron collars locked around our necks.

On the first day, one group of men had made a run for it, trying to reach the forest, which was a bowshot from the road. But, chained together, they couldn't run fast enough. A soldier's javelin had brought down their leader. They had fallen in a heap, and the soldiers had finished them off.

After that, no one tried to escape. We trudged on, mile after mile, along that road which ran straight as a spear over hills and valleys. Soon, our feet were blistered. The iron collars rubbed and chafed our necks.

Along the way, we saw villages being burned, their crops destroyed, their cattle stolen. The Romans were taking full revenge on the people who had rebelled against them.

"Where are they taking us?" That was what everyone wanted to know. Rumours spread up and down the line of prisoners. We were going to Londinium — to Gaul. We would rot in the salt mines, or break our backs in the galleys. No one knew what lay ahead, and even the strongest warriors were afraid.

On the fourth day, the road led us through a broken gateway into a city of smoke-blackened ruins. "Londinium," Conan whispered to me.

Although it was ruined, anyone could see that this had been a great city. It was 50 times bigger than our village. And our army had destroyed it! No wonder the Romans were angry.

"They will never rebuild this place," said Conan. "It's totally dead."

"Don't be too sure," said Andreas, another prisoner. "The Romans are like mushrooms. If you pick one, three more grow up in the same place."

Beyond Londinium, we were in the land of the Cantii tribe. They had not taken part in the rebellion. There were no burned villages here, no signs of war. But the towns looked more Roman than Celtic. Square stone buildings were replacing thatched huts. Many of the people wore Roman-style tunics, although they were too tall and fair to look like true Romans. "Traitors," Andreas muttered, spitting on the ground.

As we went through a town, people looked at us with embarrassment. I heard the word "slaves" being mentioned.

Conan straightened his back. "You are all slaves too!" he shouted. "Slaves of the Romans! You should have fought alongside us when you had the chance!" Then a soldier threatened him with the whip, and he was silent again.

At last, we came to a town by the sea. I had never seen the sea, although of course I'd heard of it. Travellers who passed through our village sometimes talked about it — how stormy and dangerous it was, how it could swallow ships and men. But it didn't look dangerous. It was flat and grey, and the sky came down to meet it in a long, straight line.

There was a harbour where ships were moored. I'd never seen a boat that could hold more than two people, but these ships were huge. We were herded on board in groups of 50.

"Where are they taking us?" I asked, yet again.

One of the sailors heard me and understood. "Rome," he said. "We're bound for Rome."

IV

THE SLAVE MARKET

Three months later, after a long and difficult journey, we were in the slave market at Rome. The hot sun beat down on us as we stood in line, waiting to be sold.

I couldn't understand why it was still so warm. At home, it would be autumn by now; the trees would be changing colour, and there would be chill mists in the morning. Did Rome have summer all year round? I would have asked Conan, but it would only annoy him. He hated it when I asked questions he couldn't answer — and I had plenty of those.

What would happen to us? What sort of life would we have? Would we be split up? That was what I really dreaded — being separated from Conan. I prayed that the same person would buy both of us. But praying wasn't much use, for the only gods I knew were far away. The gods of the forest had no place in this city built of stone.

The market was busy. Crowds of people had come to see the latest batch of slaves. They looked us over as if we were animals for sale. They checked that we seemed healthy, discussing us in their swift, chattering language. One of them opened my mouth and looked at my teeth. I wanted to bite his hand — but that would only bring trouble.

One at a time, each prisoner had to stand on a stone block so that everyone could see him. Then people in the crowd called out, bidding against each other. It seemed to take a long time, and I was getting hotter and hotter. I longed for a drink of water.

Then, through a gap in the crowds, I saw something very strange — a face carved on a wall, with water gushing from its mouth. It was like a woodland spring, here in the middle of the city.

"Look at that," I exclaimed, pointing it out to Conan. "How does it work? Why does the water keep on flowing?"

"I don't know, and I don't care," he replied, irritably. "You're crazy, Bryn. Still asking questions at a time like this! Can't you shut up for a minute?"

But questions were part of my nature. I couldn't stop myself staring at things — the towering buildings, the marvellous figures carved in stone, and the people. The people! There were hundreds of different faces — white, brown and black. Ordinary people were on foot; rich ones lay on beds carried by groups of slaves. Around the edges of the crowd, stallholders were selling food and drink. Children played under an archway, shaded from the sun.

Looking at all this took my mind off what was about to happen. I really didn't want to think about that.

Conan nudged me. "It's Andreas' turn," he said.

Andreas was made to stand on the block of stone. He gazed into the distance, as if he couldn't hear the voices calling out from the crowd. The final bidder was a grim-faced man, who looked as if he would be a harsh master.

I hoped Andreas would be all right. On the long journey to Rome, we had got to know him well. Although he didn't belong to our tribe, he'd become a friend.

***

My mind wandered back over the events of the last three months. The sea voyage had seemed endless. Day after day, we sailed round the edge of the Roman Empire. And I began to understand just how huge that empire was.

How could we ever get back home? Each day took us further and further away. My thoughts of home seemed to dwindle, just as the white cliffs had shrunk behind us, becoming a thin, distant line which finally vanished.

We sailed around the coastline of Gaul and Iberia — or so the sailors told us. Now and then, the ship had to find harbour, to take on fresh water or shelter from bad weather. But there was no chance of escaping. Each time, we were locked in the hold of the ship until it put to sea again.

"Don't lose hope," Conan said to me. He always knew when I was feeling bad, although I tried not to talk about it. "There *will* be a way to escape. We'll do it somehow — even if we have to go to Rome first."

We came at last to an enormous harbour. All around were ships of every shape and size. Some were preparing to sail; others were being unloaded. Up and down the gangplanks, dozens of men moved endlessly, like lines of ants. They carried sacks and bottles into the tall buildings by the dockside.

"Is this Rome?" I asked, awestruck.

But the journey wasn't over yet. We were marched off the ship, under guard, and made to walk along a busy road. A never-ending stream of ox carts rumbled down towards the port, returning filled with grain.

Then, by the roadside, I saw something that filled me with horror. There was a tall, upright, wooden cross, and a man was fixed to it by nails which had been hammered through his hands and feet. He was still alive, groaning in agony.

Andreas noticed my horrified gaze. "That's what the Romans do to thieves and murderers," he said. "They get left like that to die. Sometimes it takes days."

There was more than one cross. There was a whole row of them — a row of men, dying slowly, in dreadful pain. The people walking past hardly glanced at them, but I couldn't look away. I felt sick with fear. If the Romans treated their own people like that, what would they do to us — their enemies?

At last, in the distance, I saw what looked like snow-sprinkled hills. But I slowly realised it wasn't snow; it was a city — a vast city built over hills and valleys. The stone walls shone white in the sun. And it was *huge*. Londinium, compared to this, was like a pimple on the face of a giant.

I didn't need to ask again. This must be Rome.

Two days later, we found out why we had been brought here. There was to be a great procession to celebrate the Roman victory in Britain. We were all to be led through the streets in chains, as defeated enemies, conquered by the power of Rome.

At the head of the procession there were soldiers, rank upon rank of them. There were important-looking men in robes edged with purple. There were carts piled high with stolen things — Celtic weapons, gold necklaces, silver cups.

Sitting proudly in a chariot was the Roman leader who had caused our defeat. He was smiling, enjoying his day of triumph.

"Let his horses stumble and fall," muttered Andreas. "Let his chariot overturn. Let him break his neck! Let him lie in the gutter for the dogs to eat!"

Trumpets sounded, and the procession moved slowly forwards. Soon we were in a street, with high buildings on either side. Crowds of people watched us, cheering the soldiers and jeering at us.

"Ignore them," whispered Conan, trying to sound brave. "Walk like a warrior, not like a captive." But it's hard to walk like a warrior when you are in chains, your clothes are filthy, and you have no weapons except your pride.

The procession halted now and then for prayers and offerings to the Roman gods. These gods were made of stone. They stood in front of their houses, which were also made of stone, with stone tree trunks to hold up the roof.

Each time we stopped, I looked round. I had never imagined a place like this city. Did people actually live in those tall buildings, which were four times taller than my home? How did they get up to the top? And how could so many people find food and water? There were no woods to hunt in, no fields, no streams.

At last, the parade reached the top of a hill. There was another god here, clearly an important one, for he was huge and covered in gold. A pure white bull was led forward. The Roman leader killed it as an offering to the god.

Finally, the long day was over. We were led back to our prison outside the city.

"What will happen to us now?" I asked Conan.

He sighed. "I don't know. But somehow I don't think they will keep us here for ever."

My heart leaped up. "You mean they might send us home?"

"What would they do that for? We're their enemies, remember. If they don't kill us, they will probably keep us as slaves." Then he saw my face, and his voice softened. "Don't worry, little brother. We'll get home again one day. I promise we will."

But what use was that promise if we were separated — sold to different owners?

***

My stomach lurched as I realised that it was Conan's turn to be sold. I felt proud to see him stand there, tall, strong and seemingly unafraid. Would I be as brave when my time came?

Several voices called out, competing to buy him. Oh, I wouldn't be able to bear it if he were taken away and I never saw him again. We had been through so much together — I didn't think I could survive on my own.

The winner was the tough-looking man who had bought Andreas. He came up to pay his money and take Conan away.

This was my one chance. Even a cruel owner would be bearable if I was with Conan.

"Please," I begged him, "buy me too. Please. We're brothers. Don't split us up!"

He didn't understand my words, of course, but he must have seen the pleading in my face. He looked at Conan, then at me. The family likeness must have been obvious, although I was younger and smaller than Conan.

Too young. Too small. The man would not waste his money on me. He gave me a scornful look and turned away, taking Conan by the arm.

"No!" I cried. "Conan! Don't leave me!" I tried to follow him, but the slave dealer grabbed me roughly and shoved me back into line.

Andreas and Conan were led away quickly through the jostling crowd. Conan struggled to look back at me over his shoulder. I knew what he wanted to say to me, if only he could make himself heard in all the noise: "We have to be strong, Bryn. Don't give in. Be brave." Then the crowd closed up behind him. He was gone.

V

SOLD

Conan wanted me to be brave. So I managed to hold back my tears, telling myself I would see him again. At the first chance, I would escape and look for Conan. Somehow, I would track him down. We would run away, maybe even find our way back home.

Then I remembered how huge the city was. Conan might be anywhere among the thousands of buildings, or in the countryside round about. How could I ever find him?

I would never see him again. I was quite alone now. No father, no brother, no sisters, no mother. I wanted to crawl away and hide somewhere, like a wounded animal cut off from the herd. But I couldn't. For it was my turn to stand on the stone block, under the gaze of a hundred eyes.

Just one person looked at me with pity. One person understood how I felt. It was a little girl, 5 or 6 years old, standing near the front of the crowd. Her eyes were fixed on my face.

She tugged at the hand of the man standing next to her. She asked him something, and he answered her impatiently. With a pleading look, she asked him again. She reminded me of my sister Enid, who always felt sorry for hurt and helpless creatures. Enid would bring home a sick puppy or a bird that had fallen from the nest, and try to nurse it better, usually without success.

The man gave in to his daughter's pleading. He made a bid to buy me. No one else made a higher bid, so I was sold to him. He didn't exactly look thrilled, but the girl was pleased.

As we walked through the city, she tried to talk to me. I could tell she was asking me questions and was disappointed that I couldn't answer her. But still she talked away, pointing things out — a temple, a shop, a statue. I hardly noticed. I was walking in a kind of daze.

We came to a house, and a slave opened the door to us. The house, which looked large from the outside, was surprisingly small inside, I thought. We went through another door, and instead of being outside again, we were still in the building. Then there was an open space with trees and statues, then more of the house. I felt lost in the place.

The man shouted, and two slaves hurried towards us. He gave them some orders. The slaves led me off through a long, narrow room to another room, small and warm, with a square pond set in the floor. The two slaves cut off all my hair, which had grown long and tangled while I was a prisoner. Then they made me take off my ragged clothes. They pointed to the pond.

There were steps leading down into the water. When my foot went in, I gasped, for the water was warm. Did they mean to boil me and eat me, like barley in a pot?

I refused to get in, although the slaves yelled at me. I fought and struggled with them. Finally, one — with a sigh — stepped into the water himself, to prove that it was safe. He pretended to wash, showing me what to do as if I had never washed before in my life.

So that was what this place was for. In Rome, there were no cool, rippling streams to bathe in, like we had at home. You could only wash yourself indoors, in stale, warm water.

When I'd finished washing, I found my own clothes had been taken away. The slaves gave me a Roman tunic. I didn't want to wear it, but I was too exhausted to argue.

Without my trousers, my legs felt chilly and bare. The tunic hardly reached to my knees. It was made of pale greyish wool, very drab compared with the chequered patterns of my own clothes. And it was quite old, by the look of it. I wondered what had happened to its previous wearer. Had he died, or run away? Had he simply grown out of the tunic as he got older?

I was determined that wouldn't happen to me. I would not spend years of my life in slavery. I would escape somehow — even if I got killed in doing it.

The two slaves seemed pleased with their
handiwork. They led me through the house to a hot
room full of food smells. There was a fire burning
under a stone archway. A small, middle-aged man was
busy stirring pots of food on a ledge above the fire.

This must be the cooking place. Why did the
Romans need a separate room for everything they did?
It meant they had to walk a long way from cooking
room to eating room to sleeping room. (In a hut, like
the one I used to live in, everything you needed was
right next to you.)

The two slaves talked to the cook. It was obvious
they were talking about me and finding me funny. I
stared at the ground.

The small man beckoned me closer. Without
stopping work, he looked me up and down. He had the
sort of eyes that noticed everything but gave nothing
away. Was he another slave? He didn't behave like
one. He behaved as if he owned the place.

He ordered the two slaves out of the room. Then,
without wasting words, he pointed to the cooking pots
and showed me he wanted me to stir them. I hung
back. At home, cooking was women's work. A man
would never be seen stirring pots!

The cook spoke to me in a stern voice. I turned
away, ignoring him.

Whack! He hit me hard on the ear, almost knocking
me over. Although he wasn't much taller than me, he
had rock-hard fists and a temper as hot as his cooking
fire. He said something that sounded like: "Get on with
it — or else."

So I obeyed. I reminded myself that none of my people could see me. Conan would never know I had been made to do women's work.

All at once, I felt desperately lonely. I was in a strange place, surrounded by foreigners. I couldn't understand them; they couldn't understand me. It was like being a dumb animal. And if I didn't obey them, they would beat me like an animal, too.

I was aching with hunger. It was torture to be surrounded by food, and yet not dare to eat any of it. But the cook must have heard the rumbling of my empty stomach. He handed me a hunk of bread.

A rich meal was being prepared for the master. The cook scurried around, doing several things at once. He wanted me to chop up vegetables, but then got angry when I didn't slice them the way he wanted. He grilled some fish on a rack over the fire, cursing loudly because one of them got burnt. (Curses are easy to recognise in any language!)

When all the food was ready, it looked like a king's feast. Two serving boys carried it out of the kitchen, a few dishes at a time. The cook made me wash out the empty pots. I was very tired by now, but we still had work to do, for the household slaves had to be fed. Although there seemed to be crowds of them, later I found out that there were only 22, including me.

When I entered the slaves' eating place, every single person turned to stare at me. One or two of them tried to be friendly, but I kept my head down and said nothing. There was only one thing I wanted — a place to sleep.

Although it was dark outside, no one seemed ready to go to bed. Oily-smelling lamps gave a pale, flickering light. I longed for the warm red glow of the fire at home, and the comfort of my straw bedding.

At last, I was led to the slaves' sleeping place — a big room, high up in the house. It held a row of strange-looking objects set on wooden legs. Other slaves lay down on these things and covered themselves with blankets. Not knowing what else to do, I copied them. The thing I lay on was soft — not as soft as a heap of straw, but certainly better than the wooden deck of the ship. Why sleep up in the air, though? No use wondering, it was just one more weird Roman custom.

I wished Conan was there so that I could talk to him about the day. It had felt like the longest day of my entire life.

"I am being brave," I wanted to tell him. "I'm being as strong as I can."

Although the Romans could force me to dress like a slave and act like a slave, they could not make me think like one. I might have to learn the ways of Rome, but my heart would stay true to my own people. I promised myself that.

VI

THE MASTER'S HOUSE

After a day or two, the other slaves got used to me being there. They stopped staring at me, and they stopped trying to talk to me. Mostly, they just ignored me.

The cook couldn't ignore me, though. He got annoyed when I didn't understand his orders — and if he got really angry he would hit me. So I soon began to learn the meaning of some Roman words — they spoke a language called Latin. Slice those mushrooms... knead the dough... stoke up the fire... hurry up! The cook was always in a hurry. I could never work fast enough to please him.

Whenever I had a free moment, I thought about ways to escape from the place. It would not be easy. I couldn't climb out of a window, for all the windows opened onto the inner courtyards, not the street outside. I couldn't simply walk out of the door without the doorman seeing me.

The house was not a prison. Other slaves went out, but they always came back. Didn't they want to escape? But when I tried to leave, the doorman started asking me questions which I couldn't answer. He marched me back to the kitchen to see if the cook had sent me out. The cook got angrier than ever, and hit me again.

He wasn't always angry, though. Sometimes, if he thought I was working hard, he would reward me with extra food. Once or twice, he let me taste the leftovers from the master's table — strange things like snails, roast peacock and stuffed mice. (I much preferred bread and cheese.)

Every morning, the whole household, slaves included, gathered in the main room where the gods lived. They were three small stone figures standing on a shelf, with an altar table below them. It seemed that these were the special gods of the house, although they didn't look very impressive. The master prayed to them every day, and put an offering of food and drink on their altar.

Rome must be crowded with gods, if every house had its own little ones, as well as the huge statues I'd seen outside the temples. There must almost be more gods than people. Was this the reason the Romans were so powerful?

Later in the morning, the master's wife would come into the kitchen to give the cook his orders. She was a haughty-looking woman. Her face was always painted white and her eyebrows black. She wore lots of gold rings and necklaces. The cook was quite scared of her, which amused me.

Sometimes, the little girl came with her. When her mother wasn't looking, she would give me an anxious smile. I hope you're all right, her smile seemed to say. I hope you're not too unhappy.

There was also a son in the family, a boy who looked about 8 years old. Four people altogether — and 22 slaves to look after them. It seemed ridiculous to me. They had slaves to help them get dressed, slaves to cook their food and serve it, slaves to clean the house, slaves to attend them when they went out. Couldn't they do anything for themselves?

Of course, they were rich. The house was proof of that — it was enormous. Now and then, I caught a glimpse of the rooms where the family spent their time. There were wonderful pictures on the walls and even on the floor, made up of hundreds of little coloured stones. Then there was the walled garden, almost like another room. It had shady archways all around, and a pond where a spring of water leaped up, sparkling in the sunshine.

I explored the house gradually, getting to know my way around. The best time was the hour after the midday meal, when everyone, master and slaves, went to sleep. Everyone except me, that is. I couldn't get used to sleeping in the daytime, even though I would be dead tired by bedtime.

One day, I discovered the stable where the master's horses were kept. They were beautiful, sleek animals, not like our rough-coated ponies at home, but the sound and smell of them somehow drew me back to the old days. If I closed my eyes, I could almost imagine...

Someone spoke to me, and I jumped. The voice belonged to the slave in charge of the horses — a man of about my father's age, with skin as black as the midnight sky. He had been asleep in a shadowy corner of the stable.

Although I'd woken him up, he didn't seem angry with me. He spoke again, and I guessed somehow that he was asking me a question. When I couldn't answer, he pointed to himself and said "Tiro." Was that his name?

"Tiro," I repeated. Then I touched my own chest. "Bryn."

"Bryn." It sounded strange when he said it, but I didn't care. No one else had bothered to find out my name. (The cook shouted "*Puer*" when he wanted my attention. He used the same name for the serving boys, so perhaps it just meant "boy", "slave" or "idiot".)

Now I knew someone else's name. Tiro. I said it to myself a few times, memorising it.

Tiro was quite happy for me to look around. He told me the horses' names and let me give them some grain. I wished I could work in the stable instead of the hot, steamy kitchen.

There was a big double door, wide enough for a carriage, which must lead out into the street. But it was closed and bolted with a heavy bar of metal. Every time I went back to the stable, I hoped the door would be open. But that never happened during the hour of sleep.

***

One day, a new slave arrived. He was introduced to the rest of the household, and everyone stared at him, just as they had stared at me. But he didn't seem to care. He stared back, as if he was better than they were. He looked about Conan's age, with dark hair and a proud, handsome face.

He settled in much more easily than I did. But then, he could speak Latin. He wasn't a lowly kitchen slave like me; he was the attendant to the master's son.

Occasionally, he came into the kitchen to order a drink or some food for the boy. The cook would get it for him, grumbling loudly. But one day when the new slave came in, the cook wasn't there. He had already gone off to have his afternoon sleep, leaving me to wash up the last of the pots.

The new slave gave me an order in Latin. I shrugged, holding out my hands to show I didn't understand. He spoke louder — as if that would help! I wasn't deaf.

Speaking in my own language, I told him to get lost. I had discovered I could be as rude as I liked, as long as I kept a polite look on my face, for no one understood my words.

"Don't you tell *me* to get lost, you ignorant savage," he replied instantly, and I gaped at him. He was speaking my own language!

"Oh come on. Don't stand staring at me like a l.. witted donkey," he said. "The young master would like some..." And here, he came to a stop. He obviously didn't know the word for whatever he wanted. Or rather, he only knew it in Latin.

"How do you know my language?" I asked him. "You don't look like a Celt."

"Mind your own business," he said, looking around. "Ah, here we are." He had spotted some fruit on a shelf. (It was a type of sticky brown fruit which didn't exist in Britain, or in our language.) "Get me a plate for this, will you?"

I didn't like the way he ordered me around — after all, he was only a slave like me. But I obeyed him. It was so good to be able to talk to someone after all this time.

"What's your name?" I asked him.

"Theon."

"I'm Bryn," I said. "Where do you come from?"

"From Rome, of course."

"Did you ever live in Britain?"

"No. And I never want to, either. Now, if you'll excuse me."

He went away. The next time I saw him, I tried to talk to him. I was just being friendly, but he ignored me completely.

"What's the matter with you?" I said. Then I noticed two of the other slaves watching us. They were probably surprised to see me open my mouth — normally I was as silent as a statue.

"We can't talk now," Theon muttered. "Later, maybe."

I saw that he didn't want anyone else to know that he spoke my language. Was he ashamed of it?

The next day he came into the kitchen again when the cook wasn't there.

"Listen," he said, "don't talk to me in front of anyone else. If you do, you'll be wasting your time. I'll simply pretend I don't understand. I don't want the others to think I'm a complete barbarian."

"All right, I won't," I said. "But how did you come to speak our language?"

"My mother was a Celt. It was the first language I ever learned."

"I thought you told me you were born in Rome."

He said, "My mother was captured in one of your people's tribal wars. She was sold to a Roman slave dealer and brought to Rome. But she was always harking back to her old life. She told me all about it when I was a child. I could never understand what was so wonderful about living in a mud-floored hut. Life is far more comfortable in Rome."

"Everyone likes what they're used to," I said. I looked at him again — his black hair and dark brown eyes. "Funny. I would never have guessed that you had Celtic blood in you."

"That's because my father is Greek. I take after him. I can speak Greek and Latin," he said proudly. "Both of them are far more useful than *your* language. You should make the effort to learn Latin, you know."

"Why should I? I hate the Romans. Why should I speak the language of my enemies?"

He sighed. "You're just as stubborn as my mother. What is it with you people? Refusing to change. Living in the past. It won't do you any good."

I would have argued, but at that moment the cook came back. Theon went out without another word.

VII

A WAY OF ESCAPE

It wasn't an ordinary day. At breakfast time, the other slaves were excited. The women were all dressed up, with elaborate hairstyles. The men were talking loudly. Even the cook seemed to be in a good temper. What was happening?

It must be some kind of feast day. No one was doing much work. Everyone was getting ready to go out somewhere. One of the slaves said something to the cook, who looked at me doubtfully and then nodded.

It seemed I was to be included in the trip. Although I had no idea where we were going, I began to feel excited too. I hadn't been outside the front door since the day the master bought me.

One of the women found me a cloak to wear. Someone else gave me a small coin. I looked at it carefully — the first money I had ever owned — and the others laughed. They obviously thought I didn't know what money was.

We went out into the busy street, where everyone was hurrying in the same direction. How easy it would be to hide in this crowd, if only I could get away from the other slaves! But that might be tricky. The cook was walking right next to me, keeping an eye on me.

Soon, I saw an enormous building with many entrances. People were streaming into it from all sides. Was this the house of some god? We went in and climbed dozens of stone steps. At last we reached the top — and I gasped in amazement.

We were high up in an immense, roofless building. It was shaped like a long, narrow ship. Around the sloping sides were rows of seats which held hundreds — no, thousands — of people. Down at the bottom was an open space, long and narrow like the building, with a wall along the centre.

When we sat down, I managed to get myself next to Theon. Maybe I could ask him what was going on.

"What is this place?" I whispered to him.

"Shut up," he muttered angrily.

"I will, if you'll only tell me what's happening."

"Chariot racing," he said. Or that was what it sounded like. But how could chariots race in a place like this? There wasn't room. I must have misheard him.

I stared round at the huge crowd; was Conan somewhere among them? It was pointless trying to look for him — like seeking out one leaf in a forest. Yet I couldn't help looking and hoping.

Something was about to happen. The voices of the crowd died to a murmur. Suddenly, at the end of the open space, four great doors opened wide. Four horse-drawn chariots came charging out to race along the track.

I held my breath as they sped towards the far end. Instead of stopping, they made a tight turn and raced back along the opposite side. The drivers were incredibly skilful. Of course I'd seen chariots race before, but always in open country. This narrow track, with a sharp turn at each end, was far more dangerous.

On the third time around, the leader took the corner too close. The chariot overturned and the driver was dragged along behind the horses, frantically trying to cut himself free from the reins tied round his waist. The other chariots careered past, missing him by a cat's whisker.

The crowd loved it. They roared louder than a storm at sea, as two drivers battled for first place. The winner was the one dressed in green. This made the cook very happy, and another slave had to pay him some money.

After a pause there was another race — then another. I was starting to feel hungry now. The cook, who had won some more money, was in a very good mood. He let Theon take me to a food stall, where we bought some bread and spicy-tasting meat.

In the next race, the cook's favourite team, Green, was leading again. Then a driver in red caught up and tried to cut in on the final turn. Too close — the chariots collided. They ended up in a tangled heap of wreckage, and the White team won.

The cook was furious. He flung some money at the other slave, and then got up and stormed out. He'd forgotten all about me.

I looked around cautiously. Would anyone notice if I slipped away? Would anyone care?

When the next race began, I waited until it got really exciting. Then I slid out of my seat and made for the stairs. No one called me back, or if they did, the roar of the crowd drowned them out.

I hurried down the long stairway into the street, which was almost deserted. The whole of Rome seemed to be at the races. I'd done it! I had escaped!

Yes, great. But now what was I going to do?

***

The most important thing was to get well away from anyone who knew me. I chose a street at random and hurried along it. Then I ducked down an alley, crossed another street, and zigzagged through a maze of narrow lanes between high buildings.

I had to force myself not to rush things. It would only make people notice me. If I kept calm, there was nothing to mark me out as a runaway slave. I was wearing the kind of clothes any boy might wear, slave or free. With my pale skin and fair hair I was obviously foreign, but then Rome was full of foreigners.

After a while I came to a standstill. I had to make a plan. Where was I going?

Of course, what I really wanted was to find Conan. He was older and wiser than me. He might know how we could make the long journey back home.

But in my heart I knew there was no chance of finding him. That huge crowd at the races had reminded me just how many people lived in Rome. It would take years to search the whole city — and he might not even be there. His master might live in another town, or on a distant farm.

No. I would have to make my own way home. Maybe Conan would do the same, and we would meet on the way. Together, we would race up the hill to the village. Mother and the girls would run to meet us. "Conan! Bryn! We thought you were dead!"

Stop daydreaming, I told myself sharply. You're still a long, long way from home. What you need is to go back the way you came. Go to the big harbour and look for a ship bound for Britain.

This was easier said than done. I remembered the long walk from the harbour to Rome, but I had no idea whether we had travelled north, south, east or west. If I simply made a guess and started walking, I might head in completely the wrong direction. And I couldn't ask anyone. The few words of Latin I'd learned in the kitchen were no help at all.

At last, I decided to find the edge of the city and work my way around it, hoping to recognise the road we had walked along. I knew this plan wasn't brilliant, but it was all I could think of.

If I did manage to reach the harbour — what then? How would I know which ship was going back home?

Would I have to pay the captain to take me? Would people realise I was running away?

I had managed to escape from my master's house — that was the easy bit. It would be far harder to escape from Rome itself.

VIII

BEWARE OF THE DOG

I walked through the silent streets until my feet grew tired. The city seemed never-ending. Broad squares lined with statues... narrow streets full of shuttered shops... palace-like houses of rich people... grubby blocks of flats for the poor... and always stone pavements underfoot, stone walls on either side, and not a tree or a blade of grass to be seen.

Something else was starting to worry me — money. My one small coin, given to me to gamble at the races, would not be enough even to buy me a loaf of bread. I would need money for food on the long journey. The only ways to get it were by begging or stealing. I knew I would be useless as a beggar, since I wasn't blind, crippled or crazy. That left me with just one choice.

I was passing a row of shops, all closed. Maybe some of them had money or valuable things inside. But they all had heavy wooden shutters fixed to the pavement with locks and chains.

Then I glanced down a side alley, and spotted a small window, quite high up. It had no shutters, just iron bars in front of it. I thought I might be slim enough to squeeze between the bars and get into the building.

It wasn't easy, but I did it. As I wriggled through the gap, I thought what a fool the shop owner must be. Quietly, I climbed down into the shadowy room. I could just make out a stone counter with rows of shoes on it.

Suddenly, I heard a menacing growl and the rattle of a heavy chain. I stepped backwards — too late. A huge dog had launched itself from underneath the counter. It sank its teeth into my leg, and I screamed in agony.

The dog began shaking my leg as if it were a captured rat. Desperately, I looked around for a weapon. The only things within reach were shoes. I snatched one up and whacked the dog round the head with it.

The dog let go of my leg for a moment, just long enough for me to leap towards the window. I scrabbled my way out. The dog was barking furiously as I limped down the alley, leaving a trail of blood.

When I'd gone far enough to be sure no one was chasing me, I sank down onto a step. I looked at my mangled leg and felt faint. I had nothing to bind it up with, no way to stop the bleeding. This was stupid. After living through a battle, would I bleed to death from a dog bite?

An old woman came slowly down the street. "Help me!" I cried. Although she wouldn't understand my words, surely she would see how much I needed help.

But this was not my home village. This was the big city, where strangers were easy to ignore. After one glance at me, she walked past on the other side of the road. Then she turned a corner and was gone.

I was starting to feel dizzy. Hearing footsteps, I looked up and saw two men approaching. One was a black man who looked rather like Tiro.

"Bryn!" the man cried, sounding very surprised. It was Tiro himself. I remembered that he hadn't been at the races with everyone else. My heart filled with relief — for if anyone could help me, Tiro would.

He didn't waste any time. Lifting me up as if I weighed no more than a baby, he carried me along the street. He knocked on a door. A woman opened it, giving a little gasp when she saw the state of my leg.

Tiro took me indoors and put me down gently on a couch. The woman washed my leg — I tried not to cry out in pain — and tied strips of cloth around it. But the bleeding didn't stop. The bloodstain on the cloth spread and grew like a bright red flame.

My head swam. Dark spots seemed to float in front of my eyes. Tiro saw how scared I was. He held my hand tightly and started speaking in a low voice. He was speaking in Latin — but somehow I could understand every word.

"Father, please hear my prayer. Please let the bleeding stop. Let the wound be healed. I ask this in the name of Jesus."

I didn't know who he was talking to. There were several people in the room, but none of them looked like Tiro's father. Then I realised he must be praying to one of his gods. What kind of god would let you call him "Father"?

All at once, I realised that my leg wasn't hurting so badly. The pain had died down to a dull ache. The bright red stain had stopped spreading outwards.

"Thank you," I whispered to Tiro and his god.

Tiro said something to me in Latin. My flash of understanding, sudden and bright as lightning, had vanished. I couldn't make out a word he said.

After some time, when we were certain the bleeding had stopped, Tiro took me back to the master's house. He carried me most of the way, stopping every now and then to rest. It was lucky he was so strong.

My escape bid had been a total failure. I was determined to try again — but not yet. I would have to wait until my leg was completely healed. Also, I would make sure I had some money next time, even if I had to steal it from the master himself.

As we went in, I began to feel frightened. I would be in bad trouble. The cook would probably beat me.

All the other slaves were back by now, eating their evening meal. Everyone started talking at once. When he saw me, the cook looked relieved for an instant, then angry. He came towards me with his fists clenched.

But Tiro stood in front of me, blocking his path. Tiro was far bigger and stronger than the cook. He pointed to my injured leg, probably explaining about the dog bite. Fortunately, he didn't know the whole story.

The cook was still not happy. He started shouting. I guessed he wanted to know why I'd left the other slaves at the racetrack. If only I knew more Latin, I could have made up some excuse or other. As it was, I was helpless.

Somehow, though, Tiro managed to calm things down. I don't know what he said, but it made everyone laugh. Even the cook gave a wintry smile, and he decided not to punish me. But he watched me very closely from that day on.

***

I was allowed a few days in bed because of my leg. When no one else was around, Theon came to see me.

"I know what you were doing," he said. "You were trying to run away."

"I wasn't," I said. There was something about Theon that I didn't trust.

"Don't worry — you can tell me. I promise I won't tell anyone."

If he had been a true Celt of my own tribe, I might have believed him. But he was only half Celtish — and he couldn't even remember the name of his mother's tribe. He didn't think it mattered! That showed how much of a Celt he was.

"There's nothing to tell. I went outside to get a drink and then got lost," I lied.

"Oh yes?" His voice was mocking. "So badly lost that you ended up miles away?"

"I was trying to find my way back."

He laughed. "Back here? Or back to Britain?"

When I didn't answer, he got annoyed. "What's so wonderful about Britain? It rains all the time. The people are quarrelsome savages. The women are ugly and the food's lousy. That's what the soldiers say."

"Then why were the Romans so keen to conquer it?" I asked him.

That silenced him, but only for a moment. "I suppose we'll eventually make it worth living in. We might even make a profit out of it."

Yes — like Theon might make a profit out of me. If I confided in him, he might keep my secret, but only while it suited him. If he told the master about my plans to escape, then he might be rewarded.

On the other hand, if I did tell him, he could help me. He probably knew the answers to many of my questions. And I was desperate to talk to someone. My thoughts had been trapped inside my head for too long because I couldn't put them into words. Should I tell him?

In the end, I decided not to. At least, not yet.

IX

SATURNALIA

My escape bid had taught me something important — I must try to learn the Roman language. Without it, I would get nowhere.

Until now, I hadn't even attempted to learn Latin. I had closed my ears to the sound of it all around me. But now I started listening, and I was surprised to find that I could understand quite a bit of what people were saying. Even if I only knew some of the words, I could often make a guess at the rest.

But actually speaking Latin... that was harder. I didn't want to say something totally stupid and have people laugh at me.

The first person I spoke to in Latin was Tiro. I knew he would never laugh at my accent or make fun of my mistakes. By now, I was in the habit of visiting the stable every afternoon during the hour of sleep. If Tiro was asleep, I didn't wake him. But quite often he was awake and willing to talk.

When I asked him, he told me about his life before he became a slave. "You and me, we're not like the rest of the slaves," he said. "They were born to it — their mothers were slaves. They don't know any other way of life, and even though they grumble, they don't mind it too much."

Tiro had been born in a southern land far across the sea, so distant that his people had never heard of the Romans. He had never seen a white-skinned man, just as I, in Britain, had never seen a dark-skinned one. His tribe lived by hunting the animals that grazed on the hot, dusty plains.

I asked him what kind of animals they were, and he tried to describe them. Some sounded rather like the deer we used to hunt in the forests, but others seemed very strange. Creatures that looked like oxen but could run like horses; animals with necks as long as a spear; huge, heavy creatures with tails attached to their heads.

Was he making this up? Or was my shaky grasp of Latin making me misunderstand him? He must have seen the look of doubt on my face.

"It's all true," he said. "If you go to the Games, you'll see them for yourself."

I asked him how he came to be in Rome.

"When I was a young man, with a wife and baby son, there came a time of terrible drought. All the rivers dried up. The animal herds roamed far across the land, looking for water, and we followed them. We went into the lands of a different tribe, our enemies. But what else could we do? If we had stayed in our own land, we would have died of hunger and thirst."

There was a war between the tribes. In the fierce fighting, most of Tiro's friends were killed and the rest were captured.

"I was sold to a tribe further north. Then I was sold again to a slave dealer. I don't know what happened to my wife and baby. Probably they are dead. But if he's still alive, my son must be about the same age as you."

I understood the look of longing in his eyes. He had lost his family, and I had lost mine.

Tiro was taken to Rome — a long journey through deserts, down a river valley and over the sea. By then, he knew there was no way he could ever find his home again. He was sold in the slave market. His new master was big and fat, needing strong slaves to carry him on his couch whenever he went out.

"What was he like?" I asked.

"He was a bad master," said Tiro, scowling at the memory. "If you stumbled while you were carrying his couch, he would have you whipped. If you got old or sick, he would sell you. If you tried to escape, you'd be branded for life."

He touched a mark on his forehead. It was an old scar which I'd noticed before, three lines making a shape like this:

F

"*Fugitatus,*" Tiro said.

I asked him what it meant. He never got annoyed by my endless questions. If I didn't understand a new word, he would try to explain it, helping me to learn the language.

"It means a slave who keeps running away. So take care, Bryn. Next time, this could happen to you."

"Not me," I said.

"You mean, next time they won't catch you? That's what everyone thinks. I ran away twice. They caught me both times. My old master said that if I did it again, he'd sell me to an *ergastulum*."

Another word I didn't know. "A prison farm," Tiro explained. "They keep slaves in chains and treat them like animals. Terrible places."

"But you did get away," I said.

"Not by escaping. The old master died, and all his slaves were sold. I was lucky to be bought by Lucius, our master. He looks after his slaves. He only punishes them when they deserve it."

Maybe. But even a good master didn't make me content to be a slave. I was still determined to run away.

Hesitating, stumbling over words I didn't know, I told Tiro of my plans. Somehow, I knew I could trust him. He wasn't at all like Theon — he was a friend.

"I need money," I said. "Some of the other slaves have got some. How do they get it?"

"Oh, different ways. If I take the master's guests home in the carriage, they often give me a tip. And we all get a present at Saturnalia."

There wasn't time to ask him what Saturnalia meant. The cook was shouting for me — I had to go back to work.

***

As the months passed and my Latin slowly improved, I started to get to know the people around me. Closest to me in age were Rufus and Clemens, the two serving boys. They were quite friendly once they realised I could begin to understand their talk. I liked the two of them because they were funny. They were forever playing tricks on the cook, stealing food or hiding his favourite kitchen knife. They could each put on an innocent look, as blank as the face of a statue.

Neither of them liked Theon. He looked down on them because he thought his job was more important than theirs. Rufus could do a good imitation of Theon, giving orders as if he were the master himself.

I learned what "Saturnalia" meant — it was the next big feast. Everyone was looking forward to it. One of the women told her young son, "At Saturnalia, the slaves become masters and the masters become slaves." What did she mean by that?

I learned that the cook had a name — Quintus — and I began to understand his instructions better. He didn't shout at me quite so much. This was fortunate, for in the days leading up to Saturnalia, we were extra busy in the kitchen. We prepared special food — rich sauces, pastries, roast hare and duck, and the head of a boar. According to Rufus, this was all for the slaves to eat, not the master. I thought he was joking.

At last, the day arrived. Just like on other feast days, no one had to do much work. But Saturnalia wasn't like the other festivals. For a start, there were presents for everyone, including the household gods, who were crowned with garlands. The master gave each slave some money. I decided not to spend mine — I would save it for the day of my escape.

Rufus gave me a little cake, painted gold. "I nicked it from a baker's shop," he said proudly.

Clemens handed me three small cubes with dots on each side. I wondered what they were for. "A game," said Clemens, promising to teach me it later. Best of all, Tiro gave me some more money. I felt bad because I had nothing to give in return.

Until now, I hadn't owned anything, not even the clothes I wore. Where could I keep my money safe? In the shared dormitory, there was no place to hide valuable things. The best place I could think of was the stable, where the old walls had dozens of cracks and holes in the plaster. I wrapped the money in a piece of cloth and pushed it deep into the wall.

Everyone got dressed up ready for the evening meal. The master's wife had loaned her maid some of her own clothes and jewels to wear. The master's attendant looked very grand in a borrowed toga. All of us were given special hats to wear.

"These hats are what slaves wear on the day they're set free," said Clemens. "During Saturnalia, we're free. We can do as we like."

"But only for a couple of days, remember. Don't do anything stupid," Rufus warned me.

We all went into the master's dining room. Feeling rather nervous, I copied the other slaves and lay down on a couch beside a low table. I looked round. All the slaves were here, so who was going to bring in the food?

The answer was — the master and his wife. It was funny to see that haughty women acting as a servant. Her children helped her, bringing in dish after dish of food. There was more than anyone could eat, and plenty of wine to drink.

I saw the master's son looking at me. By now, I knew that his name was Manius. He was only a few years younger than me. The slaves didn't like him much — he was spoilt and hard to please, not at all like his little sister, Lucia.

"Are you a Celt?" Manius asked me. "Where do you come from?"

"From the Iceni tribe," I told him.

"That's not what I asked you. Do you come from Britain?"

I nodded.

"I think I will have you as my attendant," he said. "It's quite fashionable to have a British slave. Father, may I—"

"Silence, boy!" the cook yelled at him. "Servants should not speak in front of their betters. Don't you know anything?"

I wondered how he dared talk to the master's son like that. But everyone laughed. It seemed anything was allowed during Saturnalia.

One person, though, wasn't even smiling. Theon glared at me from across the room. He looked as if he would like to kill me.

I wanted to tell him not to worry — I had no desire to take over his job. But then, it wasn't up to me. I was just a slave; I had to do whatever job I was given, even if Theon hated me for ever.

Oh well... by tomorrow, Manius would probably forget the idea. I really hoped he would.

X

FINDING GOLD

We all ate far too much that night, and some people drank too much. Albus, the doorman, knocked over a whole jug of wine, which went everywhere.

"Someone call for young Manius to clean it up!" he said.

He was joking, of course. The master and his family had slipped away, leaving us to enjoy ourselves. They weren't really our slaves — it was all a kind of game.

The cook didn't eat much, but he drank several cups of wine. He had his arm around the waist of Anna, the maid, who was giggling a lot and showing off in her borrowed finery. I looked for Tiro, but he had gone out. For some reason, he didn't seem to enjoy Saturnalia as much as the others.

Rufus gave a huge yawn. "This is where it gets boring. They all get drunk and make idiots of themselves."

"Come to the dormitory, Bryn," said Clemens, "and we'll teach you how to play dice. We're allowed to gamble during Saturnalia."

They taught me the rules of the dice game, and then said we should start playing for money. But I didn't want to risk losing my small amount of cash. I'd seen Quintus win money at the races, only to lose it all.

"Oh, go on," said Clemens. "It's no fun without something to win or lose."

Rufus asked, "What are you saving your money for? Going to buy your freedom, are you?" They both laughed, but the words made my ears prick up.

"Buy your freedom — what does that mean?"

"Slaves can go free if they save up enough money to pay the master what they're worth," Rufus explained.

"But most people don't bother, because it takes so long," said Clemens. "You ask Tiro. He's been saving up for years and years, and he still hasn't got enough." I felt even more grateful for the money Tiro had given me.

Rufus sighed. "Well, if we can't play for money, let's use something else. Bryn, why don't you fetch some of those little honey cakes from the dining room? There were lots of them left."

"Honey cakes," groaned Clemens. "I never want another honey cake in my entire life."

Rufus nudged him with his elbow. "Go on, Bryn," he said to me.

I guessed that when I went out they would take the chance to look for my money. I didn't care — they could search the dormitory all night and never find it.

In the shadowy passage that led to the dining room, the cook was kissing the maid. I felt embarrassed, and walked past pretending not to see them. When I came back with a plateful of cakes, they had gone. But in the place where they'd been standing, my foot touched something. I picked it up and carried it towards the nearest lamp.

It was a gold bracelet — probably one which Anna, the maid, had been wearing. The master's wife had lent her about a dozen of them. Would she notice if one of them disappeared? The bracelet was heavy and plain, not richly decorated, like most of her jewellery. But it was gold, and gold is always valuable.

My heart was beating fast. I tucked the bracelet into a fold of my tunic. Looking round to make sure no one had seen me, I walked towards the stables as casually as I could. Tiro wasn't there. Only the horses, moving restlessly in their stalls, saw me go in and hide the bracelet next to my money.

"You took a long time," said Rufus, when I returned.

I told the boys about Quintus and Anna. They didn't seem at all surprised.

"It's Saturnalia," said Clemens, as if that explained everything.

***

The master's wife didn't appear to notice that a bracelet had gone missing. Even when Saturnalia was over, no one said anything about it. Gradually, I forgot to feel anxious over it. I stopped having nightmares about being found out and punished.

I didn't tell Tiro what I had done because I knew he wouldn't approve. There were some things Tiro would never do — stealing, lying, gossiping, or hurting people. He said his god didn't like that sort of behaviour.

I felt curious about this god of his. I hadn't forgotten the day when Tiro prayed and my leg stopped bleeding. (The wound had healed completely by now. All you could see was a line of faded scars.)

"Tell me about the gods of your people," I said one day.

Tiro looked surprised. "My people worshipped the spirits of animals. The snake for his wisdom, the lioness for her courage..."

"Not those," I said. "Who was the god you asked to heal my leg? *Father*, you called him."

Tiro said, "I prayed to the one true God, the maker of heaven and earth. There are no other gods. They don't exist, except in people's minds."

This seemed a weird idea to me.

"You really believe there's only one god? What's he like, then?"

"He's like a father," said Tiro. "He loves me as my father loved me. Whenever I talk to him, he hears me. I can't see him, but he sees me, and he knows all about me."

"How do you know? If you can't see him, how can you possibly know what he's like?"

Tiro said, "Have you ever heard of a man called Jesus of Nazareth?"

I shook my head.

"He lived in the land of Judea, far to the east. He looked like an ordinary man, but he was God's Son born on earth. He said: 'I have come to bring good news to the poor, freedom to the captives, and sight to the blind.' And he said: 'Anyone who sees me has seen God, my father.' That's how we can know what God is like."

"Where is he now, this Jesus?" I asked. "Have you met him?"

Tiro said, "He was killed by the Romans, 30 years ago. They crucified him. But he was God's Son — he was stronger than death itself. After three days, he came alive again, and many people saw him. I've talked to one of them — he's an old man now, but he remembers everything. He saw Jesus being taken up to heaven, back to God, his father."

I thought this story was very strange. And yet my mind kept returning to it. I remembered my own father — how much he loved me, how much I missed him. I almost wanted to believe in Tiro's fatherlike God, and I wished I could meet Jesus, who came to bring freedom to captives.

Freedom — I longed for it. As I kneaded the dough in the hot kitchen, or piled wood on the fire, my mind was often far away. I was back in my own country. I could go where I wanted and no one could stop me. No master could buy or sell me. No cook could order me around.

"Hey! Wake up, boy!" Quintus bellowed in my ear. "Why did I get landed with a useless idiot like you? I only hope the next one is better."

What did he mean, the next one?

He enjoyed my look of bewilderment, and then he explained: "The master has a new job for you. Starting tomorrow, you're to be young Manius' personal attendant. Nice easy work, not that you deserve it. Wipe his nose... keep him out of trouble... take him to school..."

Apart from not knowing what "school" meant, I quite liked the sound of that. It would make a change from the kitchen.

"You want to be careful," the cook warned me. "That Manius is a spoilt little so-and-so. He's bossy enough to be Emperor. Likes to get his own way all the time."

Oh yes? Look who's talking, I wanted to say. But I didn't dare. In silence, I got on with my work.

XI

LESSONS

Before sunrise, I set out with Manius and Theon for the mysterious place called school. Theon was there to teach me how to do his job. He carried a candle to light our way, while I held Manius' bag of school things. Manius, of course, carried nothing at all, yet he walked very slowly — slower than the ox carts that lumbered through the city in the hours of darkness.

"I don't want to go to school," he muttered. "It's so boring."

We came to a room which opened onto the street, as if it had once been used as a shop. Inside, a dozen young boys sat on wooden benches. Manius joined them. A tall, stern-looking man was talking, and the boys were repeating each thing he said. This went on for a long time.

"You should listen," Theon whispered to me. "He's teaching them to speak Latin clearly. Pay attention and you might lose that ridiculous British accent."

All morning, Theon and I sat on the steps outside the entrance. There were some other attendants there too, but most of them were old men. Manius was right, I decided — school *was* boring.

After the speaking lesson, each boy took out two flat pieces of wood covered in a layer of wax. The boys made marks in the wax with thin metal rods. The teacher looked at their work, praising some boys, shouting at others. When the wax was covered in little marks, it was smoothed out and the whole thing started again. Why?

When I asked Theon, he stared at me in disbelief. "They're learning to write. Those little marks — they all have a meaning, a sound. Put them together and they make words. Are you telling me there's no one in Britain who can read or write?"

"I think some of the Druids can," I said. "But not the ordinary people. Why would they need to?"

Theon said, "If you can read and write, you don't have to memorise everything. You can read what other people have written. You can send messages to the ends of the empire."

"I still don't see why a little kid like Manius has to learn it."

"He'll need it when he's older," said Theon. "Look around you. There's writing everywhere."

It was true. I had never really noticed, but the little marks were carved into the bases of statues, painted above doorways and scrawled on walls.

"Can you read and write?" I asked Theon.

"Of course. That's why the master bought me to be Manius' attendant. What *you're* meant to teach him, I can't imagine."

"Read something, then," I challenged him. "Read that." The wall opposite the school was marked in several places with those mystical signs.

"*Vote for Marcus Casellius*," Theon said. "And that says *Beware of the dog*. Oh, and this one might interest you: *Twenty pairs of gladiators will fight on 18 March, with a full programme of wild beast shows and British captives*. You should go along to see that. Wild beasts and barbarians — it might remind you of home."

I ignored this. "But how did you learn to read? You're only a slave, after all. Did you go to school?"

"No — my father taught me."

"Was your father a slave too?" I asked, curious to find out more about Theon's past life.

"Yes, but he was an important one. My father was very clever. He took care of the master's business affairs — my old master, I mean."

"What happened to him?" I asked, for it sounded as if his father was dead.

"He set off with the master on a voyage to Aegyptus. They never got there. The ship ran aground in a storm..." His voice tailed off.

For the first time ever, I felt sorry for Theon. I knew what it felt like to lose your father.

"Is your mother still alive?" I asked.

"As far as I know, she is. After the shipwreck, the master's brother inherited all his wealth. He kept some of the slaves and sold the rest of us. I don't know where my mother is now."

Exactly like me! I didn't know where my mother was either. "That's bad," I said. "You must miss her."

"Not really." Theon's voice was cold. "She was a foolish woman, a typical Celt. Even after 20 years in Rome, she was still a barbarian. Wherever she is now — even if it's the Emperor's palace — she's probably complaining that it's not like Britain."

I decided I could never be friends with Theon. We spoke the same language, and similar things had happened to us, but that didn't mean we were alike. Just the opposite, in fact.

I gave up the effort to be friendly. We sat in silence as the long morning dragged on.

When school was over, Theon showed Manius the writing on the wall. (What were *gladiators?* I didn't ask because I was tired of Theon making me feel stupid.) Manius got quite excited.

"I must ask Father if we can go. I'd love to see the British warriors. Bryn, have you ever seen gladiators in combat? It's great! They fight and fight until one of them gets killed."

"Not as good as a real battle, though," said Theon. "And Bryn has actually lived through one. You should ask him about it."

How did Theon know that? I hardly ever talked about the battle — I hated to remember it. Theon must have overheard one day when Clemens asked me how I was taken captive. I told Clemens a little about the day my father died. Clemens understood, and stopped asking questions.

But not Manius. He wanted me to tell him all about the battle. What sort of weapons did the British use? What were their chariots like? If the Romans were outnumbered, how did they win the battle? How many dead bodies did I see? Manius was too young to understand my feelings — or perhaps a slave's feelings didn't matter.

Theon smirked, and I saw he'd done this on purpose. He hadn't forgiven me for taking over his job. From tomorrow, he would be running errands for Pallas, the master's secretary. "It's a step up for me," he had boasted. "Secretary's assistant; I might be the secretary myself, one day." But I guessed he would have to work a lot harder than he was doing now.

All the way home, Manius pestered me with questions. When I didn't answer he got angry. "Don't be insolent, boy," he warned me. "If I tell my father, he'll have you whipped."

The next day, when I took him — or rather followed him — to school, Manius was in a better mood. "I asked Father, and he said that after school you can take me to see the British warriors in training," he said. "They're at the gladiator school of Decimus Lucretius Valens. Do you know where that is?"

I hadn't a clue. I still did not know my way around the city. We had to ask several people before we found our way to the gladiator school.

The training arena was a high-walled wooden structure with a few tiers of seats around the sides. We sat down amongst a small crowd of onlookers. Below us, in the sand-floored arena, two men were practice-fighting with wooden swords. They had helmets with protective face masks, and one wore body armour. The other fought in the Celtic way, with only a sword and small shield.

Watching them, I could see why my people had lost that final battle. The Briton swung his sword wide, slashing with the edge of the blade, while his opponent — probably Roman — stabbed with the sword point. On a crowded battlefield, the Roman method was better. But here, in the open, they seemed equally matched, and the Celtic fighter was very quick on his feet. Even with wooden swords, it was exciting to watch.

Obviously, I wanted the Celt to win. So did Manius. "Come on, Briton!" he yelled. "Kill him! Kill him!"

Someone shouted an order, and the fight ended. It was hard to tell who would have won if the weapons had been real. But Manius shouted, "Well done, Celt! You slaughtered him!"

The British warrior took off his helmet and face mask. He looked up at the small crowd of onlookers. Then his mouth opened wide in surprise. A huge smile spread across his face.

It was Conan! I had found my brother at last!

XII

IN THE ARENA

In the months since I saw him last, Conan had grown taller and stronger. He was almost as tall as our father had been, though not as broad-shouldered. He had also grown much more skilful with his sword.

"How did you learn to fight like that?" I asked him.

"They make us practise every day. In a few days, I'll be doing it for real." At this thought, the smile left his face. "But tell me, Bryn — are you all right? What's been happening to you?"

I wanted to touch him, to hug him, so that I could feel sure this was reality and not a dream. But he wasn't allowed to leave the arena. I leaned over the wooden parapet and we had a hurried conversation.

He told me what had happened since the day when we were sold. His first master, a farmer, had been a cruel man.

"We couldn't understand his orders at first. It wasn't our fault — but we got punished every time we made a mistake. Once, Andreas cut a tree down when the master just wanted him to trim it a bit. He got a terrible whipping for that. What's your master like?"

"All right. This is his son," I said warningly, although of course Manius couldn't speak our language. "I have to look after him."

Now Conan noticed Manius, who was gazing at him with hero worship. "Looks like real hard work."

"Oh, it is."

I was finding out that life as a slave could be quite pleasant, or it could be unbearable — everything depended on your owner.

"But what happened next?" I demanded.

"At Saturnalia, when everyone got drunk, Andreas and I ran away. We made it as far as that big port — you know, where we first landed. We wanted to find a ship sailing for home. But it was wintertime and people looked at us as if we were mad. Very few ships set sail in winter. We never thought of that."

After several days of living rough, they were captured and sold again, this time to the owner of the gladiator school. He was always on the lookout for new slaves, for obvious reasons.

"And it's not such a bad life," Conan said. "At least they feed us well, and look after us if we get sick."

"Yes, and then make you fight to the death," I said. I could hardly bear to think about it. I had found Conan, but in a few days I might lose him again — for ever.

Conan grinned at me. "You only get killed if you don't win the fight. I'll have to make sure I win, that's all."

Manius was tugging at my arm. "Talk in Latin, not your foreign language," he ordered me. "Who is this? Is he from your tribe?"

"He's my brother."

Manius was impressed. "I never knew you had a gladiator for a brother."

"Neither did I, until just now."

Before we had time to talk any more, Conan was ordered away by his master. The following day, we went back, but he wasn't allowed to talk to us. Perhaps his owner thought we were planning to help him escape.

Two days later, the Games began. No more time to practise — the next fight would be for real.

***

Holding a fan in case Manius got too hot, and a cloak in case he got too cold, I waited for the show to start. The arena below me was not much bigger than the one at the gladiator school, but the rows of seats mounted up high on all sides. Every seat seemed to be filled. Instead of sitting far back among the other slaves, I was near the front with Manius and his father. I would be close to the action, close enough to see Conan's face — maybe for the last time.

I tried not to think about that. Conan was not going to die. He would fight well, win the combat, and make everyone cheer. He would be a hero.

Yes, and afterwards? He would have to fight again soon, then again and again. Manius had told me that a few gladiators — the very skilful or very lucky ones — managed to fight on for years and earn their freedom. But most of them got killed.

Before the gladiators came on, there was a wild beast show. Several strange animals were driven into the arena, hunted down and killed. There was a massive beast with a tail at each end, a striped horse, and a cat almost as big as a man. Normally I would have been curious about these weird and wonderful beasts. But I couldn't think of anything except the gladiator fight.

Then came some men who fought with wooden weapons. Manius looked impatient. "This is just to get the crowd warmed up," he said. Two women hacked at each other using real swords, but they weren't particularly skilful. As their combat dragged on and on, the crowd grew tired of it and started shouting, "Gladiators! We want the gladiators!"

At last, in single file, the gladiators marched into the ring. There were several Britons among them. Although all their faces were covered in warpaint, I spotted Conan at once — it was something about the way he walked. Behind him, I thought I recognised Andreas.

There were 40 men altogether. If Manius was right, by nightfall only 20 of them would be left alive.

I had a sick feeling inside me. Conan could fight well, but so could the others. They had all been in training, most wore armour of some kind, and each one would be fighting for his life.

The fighters lined up facing a high seat with a canopy over it. The man who sat there, dressed in purple, must be the Emperor Nero. He was supposed to be a god. To me, he seemed like an ordinary man, youngish, and rather bored looking, as if he'd been to hundreds of these Games.

"Hail, Emperor!" the gladiators chanted. "Those who are about to die salute you!"

They marched out again. A trumpet sounded, and Manius sat up. "This is where the real fun starts," he said.

Two gladiators entered the arena. One had a large shield, a sword, armour and a helmet. The other carried only a net and a three-pronged spear.

"That doesn't seem fair," I said to Manius. "They should give both men the same armour and weapons."

"Oh, but that would be so dull. It's more interesting when the fighters have different skills. They have to use their own strength and their opponent's weaknesses. Just you watch — a good net-and-trident man will often bring down a chaser. Isn't that right, Father?"

The master smiled fondly down at his son. The boy was quite good company when he wasn't in a bossy, demanding mood.

The first fight was slow to get started. The gladiators circled each other warily, and the crowd grew restless.

Several times the chaser, as Manius called him, dodged the thrown net. The net man gathered it in again, waiting for his chance.

"Come on, you cowards!" Manius yelled. Some onlookers began booing and throwing rotten fruit. I wondered how those plump Roman shopkeepers would react if they were shoved into the arena for a life-or-death fight. I bet they would show what real cowardice looked like.

The net man threw again — too high, missing the chaser as he darted forward. The chaser's sword took the net man right in the stomach. He sank down onto the sand, blood pouring from the wound. "He's had it! He's had it!" people began to chant, holding out their hands in some kind of signal. "Kill him!"

The winner looked up towards the Emperor's throne. The Emperor made the same signal as the crowd. At once the winner slit his opponent's throat, and more blood stained the sand. The audience roared with delight.

I felt disgusted. Killing people in battle was one thing. Killing people for amusement, for pleasure — that was different. How dare the Romans call us savages? They were the savages. They were like a pack of ferocious wolves, thirsty for blood.

The winning gladiator bowed to the cheering crowd. The loser's body was dragged away, and clean sand was sprinkled over the place where he'd fallen. Two more fighters came in.

"That's what we call a mermaid man," explained Manius. "See the fishtail shape on his helmet? And the other, with the small curved sword, is a Thracian."

I didn't really care. Neither of them was my brother. But as the fight went on, I got interested in spite of myself. It was an exciting contest between two swift, agile swordsmen. They were both wounded, but bravely fought on.

Then the Thracian stumbled and fell. He lay helpless in front of his enemy, holding up one hand as if to beg for mercy. This time, many people shouted, "Let him go!"

"He fought well," the master said. "He should be allowed to live and fight again."

The Emperor must have agreed, for he gave a different signal this time. The winning gladiator sheathed his sword and helped his opponent to get up and walk away.

But that was unusual. I sat through a dozen more fights, all ending in death. Sometimes, the winner was so badly wounded that two deaths seemed likely. In between contests, there were other acts — clowns imitating gladiators, a dwarf fighting a woman, and two men wearing helmets with no eyeholes, so that they had to fight blindly.

When would it be Conan's turn? I was dreading it and yet longing for it. I wanted an end to the terror that made my heart jump each time the arena doors were opened.

If I was terrified, how must Conan feel? Down there, behind that closed door, he would see nothing. But he would hear the agonised cries of wounded men and the blood-crazed yells of the mob.

And he would have to walk out there alone. It wouldn't be like going into battle, surrounded by friends. Alone he would step out of the dark doorway to meet his enemy. I couldn't help him, no one could.

Suddenly, I remembered another time when no one could help. Tiro had prayed to his god that day, and my leg had stopped bleeding. Would the god listen to me now? If only Tiro were here.

Tiro had told me his god was like no other gods. You didn't need to stand before an altar if you wanted to pray — you could talk to him anywhere. And you didn't have to bring him offerings to make him answer you.

Silently, surrounded by the thunderous roar of the crowd, I prayed to Tiro's unseen god. "Are you there? Can you really hear me? Please help Conan. Please don't let him die..."

The trumpets were sounding again. The doors were opening. A heavily armed chaser stepped out, followed by a British warrior.

"That's him," I breathed.

"Look, Father!" cried Manius. "That's Bryn's brother down there."

"What?" The master looked startled, then angry. "Is this true? You shouldn't have brought Bryn to see his brother getting slaughtered!"

"He won't get slaughtered," said Manius confidently. "He'll win — won't he, Bryn?"

I didn't answer. The fight was about to begin.

XIII

LIFE OR DEATH

Conan and his opponent each had a sword and shield. But the enemy's shield was twice the size of Conan's, and he wore arm and leg guards, a helmet and a wide leather belt. Conan had no body armour at all.

"He's better off without it," said Manius. "All that weight will slow the chaser down."

At first, it seemed he was right. Conan was agile and quick moving. He ran rings around his opponent, attacking his unguarded side, then leaping away. The onlookers shouted their approval as his sword bit into the chaser's shoulder. "Chaser" was the wrong name for him — Conan was doing all the chasing.

"He looks like a hound attacking a great, slow ox," said Manius, admiringly.

But oxen have horns. The chaser's sword kept stabbing out at Conan — usually missing him because he was so quick. Then came a time when he wasn't quick enough. The chaser stabbed him in the thigh.

I gasped. I could almost feel the pain in my own leg, and I clenched my fists so tightly that my fingernails dug into my palms.

Conan didn't cry out, but anyone could see that the wound was a serious one. He carried on fighting, with blood pouring down his leg. He was limping now. He had lost his main advantage — his speed.

If only I could be down there, fighting by his side! But all I could do was watch, feeling sick with fear. Oh, Conan...

"Come on! Come on, Briton!" Manius yelled. "Keep moving! You can do it!"

The chaser advanced, driving Conan back. Conan fought fiercely and drew blood again, but the enemy hardly seemed to flinch. I could see my brother was losing strength.

Many people around us were cheering for the Briton. I shouted too — not that he could hear me. By now, he had his back to the arena wall. Desperately, he fended off his attacker's sword strokes. He had lost his shield and was using his sword two-handed.

"Aaah!" A great cry went up from the crowd. Conan had hurt his attacker again — his sword hand was bleeding. The chaser drew back a few paces.

But Conan didn't have the strength to pursue him. He looked unsteady on his feet. His sword slipped from his grasp. Then his whole body seemed to crumple, and he fell in a heap on the arena floor.

"He's had it! He's had it!" the audience chanted.

His opponent came forward with sword raised. I turned away, blinded by tears. But Manius said, "Don't lose hope. He's still alive... maybe the Emperor will be merciful."

I looked around, seeing many hands making the "death" sign, but almost as many signalling "life". Frantically, I waved my own arm in the air, shouting, "Let him go! Let him go!"

It was the Emperor who would make the decision. I'd heard he was a cruel man, who cared for no one but himself. People even said he had ordered the killing of his own mother.

What would he decide? Oh God, please let him choose life, not death!

The Emperor looked round at the excited crowd, as if he was wondering what would please them. Whatever choice he made would delight half the audience and enrage the other half. He seemed undecided. The crowd yelled even louder.

Slowly, the Emperor rose to his feet. He appeared to like the fact that everyone was watching him. Then, at last, he held up his hand, signalling for mercy. "Let him go!"

I felt like dancing with joy, until I looked back at Conan. His skin was as pale as white marble. He pressed both hands against his wounded leg, as if the pain was too much to bear. He couldn't walk — he had to be carried out of the arena.

The master said, "He may live. They have skilled doctors at the gladiator school."

"We'll go and see him tomorrow," said Manius.

I wanted to go now — at once. But of course I couldn't. I had to stay with my master, watching the rest of the Games. I saw Andreas fight, but I couldn't manage to cheer him on, or feel excited when he won. All I could think about was Conan.

When we got home, I went to Tiro and told him everything.

"I prayed to your god, and he answered me. Conan didn't get killed," I said. "But he was badly wounded. Will you come with me tomorrow and pray for him?"

Tiro said, "I can't come tomorrow. I have to drive the master to Ostia. But I can still pray for your brother, and I'll ask my friends to pray too."

Tiro had already told me that he had friends who believed in the same god — Christians, they were called. They didn't go to a temple to pray, but met in people's homes. It was all rather secretive. Tiro never mentioned his friends' names or addresses. That would be dangerous, for the Emperor hated the Christians, who refused to worship him as a god. Several Christian leaders had been killed on the Emperor's orders.

I asked Tiro if I could go with him when he met his friends. I wanted to be there when they prayed for Conan. Tiro gave me a thoughtful look, and then nodded.

"But you mustn't tell anyone where we go. Do you understand, Bryn? Not *anyone*."

We set out after Manius was in bed. By now, most people were indoors. Shops and market stalls were closed for the night. The dark streets were empty, except for a few delivery carts rumbling along. Even so, Tiro made sure we stayed in the shadows.

We turned down a side street, and suddenly I realised where we were.

"Isn't this where you brought me when the dog—"

"Shh," said Tiro.

He stopped outside a door, where he knocked three times, paused, and then knocked again. Someone opened a shutter in the door and looked out at us. "It's Tiro. Peace be with you," Tiro whispered. "And I've brought a friend."

The door was opened just wide enough to let us in. Then I heard it being bolted behind us. All this secrecy made me feel rather nervous. I began to wish I hadn't come.

But once we were inside, there was a warm welcome from the woman of the house. She remembered me from the day of the dog bite, and was pleased to see how well my leg had healed up. She led us into a well-lit room, full of people. Several of them came to greet us.

"This is a friend of mine, a seeker after truth," said Tiro. "He would like us to pray for his brother."

So I found myself telling the whole story. Before I had finished, a feeling of despair swept over me like a bitter north wind. What if it was too late to pray? What if Conan was already dead?

The room grew silent. Then several people prayed for Conan. They spoke in different accents — Greek, Roman, Jewish, African — but all of them talked to their god like Tiro did, as if talking to a father who loved them. As if God was right there in the room, hearing every word.

I liked listening, but I didn't feel I could join in their prayers. Although their God had helped me, I didn't know him like they did. I only had one father, and he was dead.

After the prayers, the Christians sang for a while. Then one of the men started telling a story, and everyone listened. It was about the man called Jesus of Nazareth, who said he was God's Son born on earth. He did amazing things — healing a blind man, and feeding thousands of people with just a few loaves of bread. Naturally, if he was the son of a god, you would expect him to have special power. That bit made sense all right, but what about this?

"Jesus began to tell his friends that he was going to be rejected by everyone. He would be put to death."

Why? If he knew that was going to happen, why didn't he escape, or call down fire from heaven to burn up his enemies? That's what I would do if I had the power. I would burn up the whole of Rome — except, of course, for Tiro and his friends. I couldn't understand why this Jesus would have let himself be killed.

After a while, the Christians started praying again. They prayed for the Emperor (which seemed strange — didn't the Emperor hate Christians?). There were long prayers for people and places I'd never heard of. It was very boring.

"Bryn, wake up!"

I opened my eyes. I don't know how long I had been asleep, but the gathering was over. People were leaving the house quietly in ones and twos, hoping not to be noticed.

"Up you get," said Tiro. "It's time to go home."

XIV

THE BEST PRICE

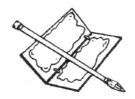

The following day, I longed for school to be over, even more than Manius did. Afterwards, we went straight to the gladiator school, which was very quiet. The practice arena was empty.

"The winning gladiators probably had a big feast last night," said Manius. "I expect they all got drunk."

I didn't care about the winners. It was one of the losers I wanted to see.

Manius knocked at a side door. It was answered by a hefty, scar-faced man, who looked as if he had been a gladiator long ago. "What do *you* want?" he growled.

Manius tried to look grown-up and important. "We have come to see one of the British warriors, the one who got wounded yesterday."

"They all got wounded. Which one do you mean?"

I said, "His name's Conan. He's my brother. Is he... is he still alive?"

"Yes, but that leg of his doesn't look too good."

The big man stood without moving, blocking the doorway. Finally, Manius realised what he wanted — money. When Manius had given him a few coins, the man suddenly became more helpful. He led us down a corridor, unlocked a door, and showed us into a small, dark room with a barred window.

Conan lay on a narrow bed. When he saw us, he smiled weakly, tried to sit up, but then gave a gasp of pain and sank down again. I saw he was still very pale — he must have lost a lot of blood. And, despite his attempt at smiling, he had a weary, defeated look about him, which reminded me of the day when we lost the great battle.

"What happened yesterday?" Manius demanded. "You lost. I wanted you to win!"

Conan didn't anwer. At first I thought he hadn't understood the Latin words.

"Tell him what I said," Manius ordered.

I began to translate it, but Conan interrupted me. "I heard. I'm not stupid," he said in Latin. In our own tongue, he added, "Just like you, little brother, I've had to learn the language of the enemy."

"Answer me," said Manius, looking impatient. "What happened yesterday? I thought you couldn't lose!"

"Well, it seems you were wrong," Conan said wearily. "Things don't always go the way you want. You'll find that out as you get older." He spoke better

Latin than I did; perhaps he'd been forced to learn faster.

"But you're still alive — that's what matters," I said. "How's your leg?"

Manius said, "Can I see it? Did it bleed a lot?" He was disappointed when Conan wouldn't unwrap the bandage on his leg.

"The doctor said it might take months to heal," Conan said, gloomily. "He said I might walk with a limp for the rest of my life." I could see how much he dreaded that. He had always been so fit and strong, proud of being the fastest runner in the village.

I tried to reassure him. "The doctor doesn't know everything. Your leg could heal up all right. Especially if I get my friends to pray for you—"

"When are you going to fight again?" Manius interrupted.

"Never," said Conan bleakly.

"But you're a gladiator," said Manius. "You *have* to fight."

Conan said, "The doctor told Decimus, my master, that it would take a long time to heal me. And the master said, 'I'm not wasting time and money on a half-trained barbarian. There are plenty more where he came from. Patch him up a bit and I'll sell him. He's fit enough to do farm work.'"

"But that would be such a waste!" cried Manius. "You're a fighter, not a farmer. You're really good at it."

"Not good enough," Conan muttered. "I lost — and Decimus doesn't like losers. Anyway, if I end up crippled I can't fight, can I?" He looked utterly miserable.

"At least they can't kill you on a farm," I said.

"Oh yes they can. They can kill you with hard work, and punishment, and beatings. It would be better to die in the arena — at least it would be over quickly!"

"Don't talk like that," I begged him. "Don't give up hope. I don't want you to die."

He turned his face to the wall, trying to hide his feelings. But I could tell just how hopeless he felt. "Go away," he said, quietly. "I'm tired."

"No. I won't leave you."

But the doorman came in and made it plain that we couldn't stay any longer.

I felt terrible, seeing Conan like that — so hopeless and miserable. It wasn't like him at all. He was my big brother. He had always been ready to help me, encourage me and stand up for me.

Now it was his turn to need help. I had to do something. But what?

Late in the night, as I lay awake worrying, an idea came to me. Conan's master wanted to sell him. Fine — I would buy him. Then I would set him free.

Yes! I sat up in bed, full of excitement. That gold bracelet was still hidden in the stable. How much would it be worth? As much as Conan's life?

I would have to be careful, though. No one must see me with the bracelet. Although I didn't think of it as stolen property — I had *found* it, after all — the master's wife might think differently.

Also, would I be allowed to buy Conan? Could a slave buy another slave? How exactly did you go about setting someone free? Where would Conan live until his leg was fit to walk on?

This wasn't going to be easy. It might even be dangerous — but I had to try.

***

On the way to school next day, and on the way home, I kept my eyes open. I saw several shops that sold jewellery — in fact, there was a whole street where most of the shops belonged to goldsmiths. Surely one of them would buy the bracelet.

The problem would be how to go there without Manius. He wasn't stupid. Although he might not recognise the bracelet as his mother's, he would certainly want to know where I got it.

I asked him if we could go back to visit Conan, but he wasn't too keen. Now that Conan was no longer a gladiator, Manius had rather lost interest in him.

"You can go while I'm in school," he said. "Just make sure you're back in time to take me home."

Perfect! That would give me some time on my own.

Later, while Tiro took the horses for exercise, I sneaked into the stable to get the bracelet. For a horrible moment, I thought it had disappeared. But it had simply slipped deeper into the hole in the wall.

I took it out and admired it, feeling the weight of it. To me, it looked like solid gold, but then I was no expert. I didn't know how much it might be worth.

Sliding it onto a length of cord, I tied it around my neck so that it hung down inside my tunic. I could feel it lying heavy over my heart.

All the way to school next day, I was nervous, but Manius didn't seem to notice. When the lessons started, I set off in the direction of the gladiator school. Then I doubled back to the street of the goldsmiths. I walked along the row of shops, trying to decide which one to visit. Who would give the highest price? Who would ask the fewest questions?

In the end, I chose a small shop that was tucked away round a corner. The two men behind the counter looked as if they might be brothers. I thought this was a good omen.

"Do you buy gold, as well as sell it?" I asked them.

"Of course. What do you want to sell?"

Looking around to make sure no one was watching, I took out the bracelet. The two brothers examined it, weighed it carefully, and talked together in a foreign language that I didn't recognise.

"Where did you get this?" one of them asked me.

My heart beat faster. "I... er... just found it. Ages ago, at Saturnalia."

I wasn't sure if they believed me. But the older one said, "We will buy it for 100 denarii."

"It's worth far more than that," I said indignantly. "I won't sell it for less than 500." I couldn't even guess how much it was really worth. I just knew I had to get the best price I could.

We argued for a while. At last, we agreed on a price — 300 denarii. I had no idea if that would be enough.

Maybe I could have got a better price by asking around the different shops, but I was still feeling nervous. It was better not to be noticed by too many people.

The younger brother counted out the money. Seeing I had nowhere to put it, he gave me a leather pouch to tuck inside my belt. "And next time you... er... *find* something, you come to us, yes?"

They obviously thought I was a thief, but this didn't seem to bother them.

I hurried out of the goldsmiths' street. Suddenly, I heard a shout.

"Hey, Bryn! What are you doing here?"

Oh, no. It was the last person I wanted to meet... my enemy, Theon.

XV

FREEDOM

"You're supposed to be attending Manius," said Theon. His voice sounded accusing. "What are you doing here?"

"Manius said I could go to see my brother," I said. (By now, the whole household knew about Conan, although I'd only told a few people. Slaves are terrible for gossiping.) "What are you doing here?"

"Taking a message for Pallas. This isn't the way to the gladiator school," he said suspiciously.

"I got lost."

Theon sighed. "Typical! Do you want me to take you there?"

I tried to sound suitably grateful. "If you could just point me in the right direction..."

But he took me right to the door, as if to make sure I hadn't lied about where I was going. He was still suspicious of me, I could tell. What would happen if he went back to the street of goldsmiths and started asking questions?

Trying not to think about this, I knocked on the gladiators' door. "I want to see the owner," I said to the doorman.

"Oh, do you now?"

"It's about my brother. Please can I talk to the master? Look, I'm sorry, but I haven't any money to give you." I wasn't going to waste my precious money on him. I might need every bit of it.

"All right, I'll ask," the man said, grudgingly. "Wait there."

I had to wait in the street for ages. At last, the door opened again. The doorman led me to a richly decorated room, very different from Conan's dark cell. It looked as if the owner of the gladiator school had made a lot of money out of it.

Decimus, the owner, was a tough-looking man. His face and arms showed the scars of many fights. At his feet lay a dog which looked even fiercer than he was. It bared its teeth in a snarl.

"Don't worry about Brutus," he said. "He's all mouth — he wouldn't hurt a fly. You wanted to see me?"

"Yes." Because I was nervous, I couldn't think what to say next. My hard-earned knowledge of Latin seemed to vanish like dew under a hot sun.

"It's my brother. I want to buy him," I managed to say.

"Your brother... now which one might he be? All you Celts look alike to me."

"His name is Conan. He has a wounded leg."

Decimus was looking me up and down. "A pity you're not a few years older," he said. "I could have used the two of you as a double act. The barbarian brothers... the crowd would love it. I would pit you against those African twins I bought the other day."

"I'm not for sale," I said.

He laughed. "Oh, any slave is for sale if the price is high enough."

"All right," I said, "how much do you want for Conan?"

"I want 600 denarii."

My heart sank. But maybe he expected me to argue about prices, like the goldsmiths did.

"I'll give you 100," I said.

"What, only 100? I could easily get 500 for him at the slave market."

"Not with his bad leg," I objected. "It might never heal right, the doctor said."

"Well, 450, then," said Decimus, grinning. It was like a game to him, and the winner would be the one who got the best bargain.

But it wasn't a game to me. I only had 300 denarii, plus a few small coins still hidden in the stable. If I couldn't bargain the price down low enough, I couldn't rescue Conan.

"I'll give you 150," I said, as firmly as I could.

After a lot of haggling, he came down to 350.

"All right, 300. I can't give you more because I haven't got it. See?" I emptied the bag of coins onto his table.

"Sorry. That's not enough," he said, turning away.

Suddenly, I was furious, and anger gave me words. "Why won't you sell him? You don't need my money because you're rich already — rich and free. Don't you remember what it was like being a slave?"

He gave me a startled look. Of course, I was only guessing, but if he had been a gladiator in the past, then probably he had been a slave.

"I remember all right," he said, his voice as sharp as a blade, and the dog growled. There was a long moment of silence.

"Very well then. You can have him for 300," he said at last.

He called for his secretary, who wrote something down and gave the writing to me. (Not that I could read it. If Decimus wanted to cheat me, the writing might say absolutely anything, such as *Vote for Marcus Casellius* or *Beware of the dog*.)

The doorman took me down to Conan's room. I told Conan what I'd done, and he stared at me in amazement.

"But where did you get the money?"

"Ask me later. Are you all right? Can you walk?"

Leaning on my shoulder, Conan managed to hobble painfully along the corridor. He could hardly put any weight on his injured leg.

The doorman was grinning as he let us out into the street. "Now be sure to obey your new master," he said to Conan. "Otherwise, he may beat you."

"I'm not your master," I said hastily. Conan would absolutely hate that idea. "I'll set you free just as soon as I find out how to."

"Free..." Conan said, looking rather dazed. He stared around at the busy street. His hand tightened on my shoulder, as if he was about to lose his balance. "Where are we going? Is it far?"

Oh, help! I hadn't given much thought to that. My mind had been set on rescuing Conan, without considering what he would do afterwards.

Until his leg began to heal, Conan would need food, rest and somewhere to sleep. Would my master allow him to stay with me? He might, if Manius asked him. But the cook might object to feeding an extra person who didn't belong to the household. I had a little money, enough to buy food for a few days. When that ran out, what would Conan live on?

Soon, though, I realised that the master's house was too far away — Conan would never make it. I took as much of his weight as I could, but he could only walk a few steps at a time. His mouth was tight with pain.

"Stop," he gasped as we came to a fountain. "I need to sit down."

Conan sank down onto the stone rim of the pool. He looked as if he couldn't walk much further.

It was up to me now. I had to be the strong one — the big brother, the decision-maker. Conan was depending on me. But what were we going to do?

Gazing around, I saw that we were in a quiet side street, not far from where Tiro's friends lived. They might help us. Anyway, it was worth a try.

"Where are we going?" Conan asked again.

"To the house of some people I know." I suddenly realised that I didn't even know their names. "They're Christians. They helped me before, when I—"

"Christians!" Conan looked alarmed. "I've heard about them. They're weird. They live off the flesh of dead people."

"No they don't," I said, certain that Tiro would never do such a thing, although I couldn't be so sure about his friends. After all, I had only met them twice. "They're nice people. They'll help us... I hope."

But as we made our way slowly down the street, I began to feel anxious. Before, when I came to the Christians' house, I was with Tiro. If I arrived without him, would they let me in? Would I even be able to find the right house?

Then I spotted something. On the wall above one door was a small drawing of a fish, just an outline, like a child might draw in mud with a stick. A fish! That was one of the secret signs the Christians used.

I tapped on the door as Tiro had done — three knocks, a pause, and then another knock. But no one answered. My heart sank like a stone.

"Hey, there!" a woman called from across the street. "Are you looking for Crispus and Marcella? They're at the shop — the baker's shop, just around the corner there."

Leaving Conan on the doorstep, I ran round the corner. The baker's shop was just closing for the afternoon sleep. Tiro's friends were fastening the shutters. They were surprised to see me, and even more surprised to hear about Conan.

"He's free? That's wonderful!" said the woman, Marcella. "God answered our prayers."

This irritated me slightly. After all, I was the one who had rescued Conan, wasn't I?

I said, "Yes, but his leg is still bad. He can hardly walk. Could he... could he stay with you, just for a few days? Until his wound heals, I mean? I can pay for his food."

"Of course he can stay," said Crispus. "Where is he now?"

"Er... he's on your doorstep."

Together, we managed to get Conan into the house. With an exhausted groan, he collapsed onto a couch. Marcella brought him a drink. He seemed to have forgotten his suspicions about Christians, for he drank it eagerly, lay back and shut his eyes.

"Don't you worry," Marcella said to me. "We'll look after him."

Look after him... Suddenly, with a horrible shock, I remembered about Manius. School must be over by now — I would be in big trouble.

As I expected, the young master was furious. Although he knew his way home perfectly well, he had waited for me outside the empty schoolroom, getting angrier with every passing moment.

"So, this is what happens! I treat you kindly, I let you go off and visit your brother, and you don't come back for hours! It's true what they say — slaves don't appreciate kindness. They only learn from the whip!"

I couldn't explain what I'd been doing, so stayed silent. He told his father what I'd done. That night I got a beating, with a warning of worse to come if I didn't do my job properly.

But I didn't care. Conan was safe — which was all that mattered.

XVI

PLANS

Conan stayed with Crispus and Marcella for almost a month, as his leg wound slowly healed. I visited him whenever I could. One day I found him sitting on the doorstep with Philo, Marcella's young son. He was teaching Philo to play knuckle-bones.

"Your friends are at the shop," he said to me. "They left me in charge. They treat me like one of the family. But I'm a complete stranger to them, not even from the same tribe. Why are they doing it?"

"Because they're Christians. See? You were wrong about them. Have you ever seen them eating dead people?"

"Not while I've been watching," Conan admitted.

Crispus and Marcella weren't rich, like my master. At first, I gave them the money I'd been hiding, to help pay for Conan's food. But when my money ran out,

Marcella told me not to be anxious. "The brothers and sisters will take care of that," she said.

I guessed she meant the Christians. They were mostly working people, or slaves, but Tiro had told me they often gave money to help people in need. "It's what the master tells us to do," he said.

It was confusing. Sometimes when he said "the master", he meant our owner, Lucius. At other times, he meant Jesus of Nazareth. I asked him what he would do if his two masters told him to do different things — for instance, if Lucius told him to stop following Jesus.

"I would obey the one I love best," said Tiro. "Lucius bought me with money, but Jesus bought me by giving up his own life."

"I don't understand."

Tiro said, "Jesus came to earth knowing he was going to be killed. He let his enemies capture him. He didn't stop them from crucifying him. Have you ever seen anyone crucified?"

I nodded, remembering the line of crosses I had seen on the very first day I had arrived at Rome. Being crucified meant a horrible, slow, agonising death, sometimes lasting for days.

Tiro was silent for a moment. He said, "Jesus' death was like a sacrifice... the greatest sacrifice ever."

I knew what a sacrifice was. If you wanted to please the gods, or turn away their anger, you could give them one of your best animals. The priests would kill it as an offering. Some religions used humans as well as animals, although that was not allowed in Rome.

Tiro said, "Because Jesus died, we don't need to make sacrifices to please God. If we believe in Jesus, we can come near to God at any time. We can know his love, like children know the love of their father."

Part of me longed to have faith like Tiro had. It would be good to feel so sure of God's love.

But another part of me didn't want to know. I didn't like the idea of Jesus as my master. I wanted to be free, with no one telling me what to do. Having Manius ordering me about was more than enough.

Oh, and talking of freedom — I discovered that it was quite simple to set Conan free. "Some owners make a big ceremony of it," Crispus told me. "But you don't have to do that. You can just say, 'I set you free', as long as you do it in front of other people. Marcella and I will be your witnesses, if you like."

So I said the words, feeling rather silly: "Conan, I set you free."

"Oh, thank you, master." He smiled, and made a mocking bow.

This was the only time he actually thanked me for what I'd done. He didn't like having to be grateful to me — his kid brother. He seemed to find it embarrassing.

But his attitude towards me was changing. He treated me more like an equal these days. Instead of telling me what to do, he would ask what I thought about things. I liked that.

"What will you do with your freedom?" Marcella asked him.

I already knew what he would say. "I'm going home," he said. "Home to Britain."

"But it's such a long way," said Marcella anxiously. "Right on the edge of the empire. Will you be able to walk that far? Your leg hasn't healed properly yet. And Bryn will really miss you — so will we." Marcella and Crispus had grown fond of Conan in the time he had been staying with them, and his news came as a shock to them.

"Oh, I don't plan to walk it," said Conan, ignoring their anxiety — and not looking at me. "I'll go by sea. It's spring now, the time when ships set sail. How much will it cost to sail to Britain?"

Crispus and Marcella had no idea. But they talked to a friend of theirs, a cart driver, who often travelled to the harbour at Ostia. Conan rode down with him to find out what he could.

When he returned, he came to see me outside Manius' school. (It didn't matter if Manius saw him. I had explained that Conan's master had set him free — I just didn't mention that the master happened to be me.)

Conan was looking depressed.

"I only found two ships sailing for Britain. One of them isn't taking passengers. The other one is, but it's far too expensive. Especially for two of us." For of course I meant to go too, though no one knew that apart from Conan. We had managed to keep our plans a secret from everybody.

He said, "There's only one thing to do. I'll have to walk. I'll take it slowly and hope that my leg doesn't give me too much trouble." He lowered his voice, even though we were speaking Celtic. "Are you with me?"

"Yes, of course. But how can we find the way?"

"I talked to some sailors. They said if we keep going northwards and westwards, eventually we'll come to the far coast of Gaul. Then there's a short sea crossing to Britain — less than a day."

He made it all sound so easy. But I knew it would be a long, exhausting journey... dangerous, too. Robbers might attack us in the mountains. I might be captured and punished for running away. We might get lost and walk far in the wrong direction.

"We're going to need money to buy food," said Conan. "Quite a lot of money — we could be on the road for months. Can you get some from the same place as last time?"

I knew what he meant — steal something. But I didn't feel too keen on that idea. Tiro always said it was wrong to steal.

"I don't know," I said. "It could be risky. Why don't we just wait until I can save up some money?"

"But that could take months — years. I can't wait that long. I've got to get out of this city! I can't stand the stinking place."

He was right; the city did stink. As the weather grew warmer, the smell, like a village dunghill, was getting more noticeable. But it wasn't just the smell that bothered him. Conan hated Rome, and everything Roman. Although Crispus and Marcella had been good to him, he couldn't forget that they were Roman too. He would be happy to leave their house.

For me, it was different. I didn't feel as bitter as Conan, but then my time in Rome had been much easier than his. I hadn't been badly mistreated, or forced to fight for my life. Of course I wanted to go home, but I also felt there was no need to hurry.

And I knew there was someone I would really miss — Tiro. To leave him would be almost as bad as leaving my own family. I couldn't even tell him what we were planning to do. Conan insisted on that, for he thought Tiro might try to persuade me to stay.

Perhaps I could ask Tiro to run away with us? But no, he would never do that. He had told me that after he became a Christian, he stopped trying to escape from his master. Instead, he worked hard and saved up his money in the hope of buying his own freedom. In another year or two, he might have enough.

In any case, Tiro would never feel at home in Britain. Even the mild Roman winter had felt chilly to him. He would hate our cold, wet, foggy weather.

But it was hard to talk to him of Conan's plans, remembering to say "he", not "we", and pretending to feel sad that Conan was leaving. Did Tiro guess the truth? He never asked me. I don't think he wanted to know.

XVII

NO GOODBYE

"Where does the master keep his money?" I asked Clemens, trying to sound casual.

"In the strongbox in his study," said Clemens. "Haven't you ever seen it?"

I shook my head. "I thought we weren't supposed to go in there."

"We aren't," said Clemens, grinning. "But if you happen to wander in there during the hour of sleep, who's to know?"

Rufus said, "Are you thinking of helping yourself to some cash? Because you needn't bother. There's only one key to the strongbox, and Pallas takes care of it." Everyone knew that Pallas, the secretary, was fiercely loyal to the master — he probably slept with the key under his pillow.

"Why do you want to know?" Clemens asked me.

"I told you: Bryn's planning a robbery," said Rufus.

I felt my face start to go red. The only thing to do was to make a joke of the whole thing. "That's right. I'm going to run off to Britain with the master's strongbox!"

"Then you'll need the strength of Hercules," said Clemens. "That box is made of metal and chained to the floor."

Rufus said, "If I wanted to steal something, I'd forget the money. There's so much other stuff just sitting around asking to be taken. See that carved ivory figure?" He pointed to a little statue in a niche on the corridor wall. "That must be worth quite a bit. And the big Greek vases in the dining room..."

"Don't be stupid," said Clemens. "How would you get them past the doorman? Small things are better. I'd have that silver statuette of Mercury from the atrium."

"Would you? How very interesting," said Theon. He had appeared round the corner of the passage and walked right in on our discussion. "I wonder if the master knows of your new interest in art collecting."

"I was only joking," Clemens said, hastily.

"Joking? Of course you were," Theon said, in that hateful, smooth voice of his. He smiled at us and strolled away.

"I hate Theon," Rufus muttered. "Always hanging around, listening in on other people."

"Because he hasn't got any friends of his own. No one likes him," Clemens said loudly. Theon must have heard this, but he didn't even turn his head.

I wondered how much of our conversation he'd overheard. He could have been listening around the corner for ages. Had I said anything that Theon could use against me?

Next day, when Conan met me outside the school, I told him what had happened.

"Then it's time we made a move," said Conan. "We'll leave tomorrow."

"Tomorrow!" I gasped. I felt it was too soon. I wasn't ready.

"Or have you changed your mind? Maybe you want to stay here. Maybe you're a Roman now, not a Celt," he said, mockingly.

"No! I do want to go. It's just that I haven't had a chance to say goodbye to anyone."

Conan looked alarmed. "Forget saying goodbye. We don't want anyone to guess what's going to happen — not even Tiro. So just act normally. Take Manius to school tomorrow, and then slip away. I'll meet you at the corner there."

This was a sensible idea. It meant I would be able to leave the house without anyone suspecting me. But I longed to see Tiro just one more time. And what about money?

"I still haven't managed to steal anything," I said.

"Just take whatever you can find tomorrow," said Conan. "But be careful. Don't get caught."

I decided to steal the little ornament that Rufus had pointed out. It was carved out of ivory in the shape of a horse and rider. The carving, which was beautifully detailed, looked foreign somehow. Perhaps it had been made in a far-away land, then brought to Rome by traders and sold for a high price.

I wouldn't take it until the last possible moment. Eventually, someone would notice the empty shelf — but if the gods were with me, I would be well out of reach before that happened.

If the gods were with me... There was one god who definitely would not approve of my plan — Tiro's god. But I pushed that thought to the back of my mind. I *had* to steal something. How else could we get money for our journey?

Waking up early next morning, I slid out of the dormitory before anyone else had even stirred. No one saw me take the ivory figure from the shelf. It was small enough to slip easily into Manius' leather schoolbag.

Although I was far too nervous to feel hungry, I forced myself to eat a good breakfast. It might be a long time before my next proper meal. Looking around, I realised that if all went well I would never see any of these people again. I would miss Rufus and Clemens. And Tiro — where was Tiro?

When I asked, Pallas said, "He drove the master to Laurentum yesterday. They'll be back tonight."

So there was no chance of seeing Tiro again. Well, perhaps it was better that way.

Manius and I left the house as usual. By now, there was no need for a candle to light our way, for the days were getting longer. Conan was right — we shouldn't delay. Summer would be the best time of year for our journey.

"Why are you walking so fast?" Manius complained. "There's no hurry. You know I don't like school."

I slowed my pace a little, wondering just how much time I had before someone noticed the missing statue. When they did notice, who would get the blame for it? Theon might report what Rufus had said. Rufus would deny everything, and probably put the blame on me.

At last, we reached the school. I gave Manius his writing things, keeping hold of the bag — it might come in useful on the journey. I sat down in my usual place on the steps outside. As soon as the lessons were under way, I got up again. "Just going to the toilet," I muttered to one of the other attendants.

Conan was waiting at the corner of the street. He looked relieved to see me. I showed him the ivory carving.

"I know someone who'll pay good money for it," I said.

"Do we have time?" Conan asked. "Maybe we should take it with us and sell it later. I've got a bit of money already — Crispus gave me some."

"If we sell it in Rome, we'll get a better price," I said.

Conan didn't argue, even though I could see he just wanted to get out of Rome immediately. He let me lead him to the street of goldsmiths, and the shop where I'd sold the bracelet.

The two brothers remembered me. They came forward, all smiles, but when I took out the ivory horseman, the smiles turned to frowns.

"Sorry. We do not buy ivory," the older one said.

"Only silver and gold," said his brother. "Ivory is no use to us. We can't melt it down and make new, you see."

"But it must be very valuable," I said. "Look how fine the carving is. I bet there isn't another like this in the whole of Rome."

The brothers raised their eyebrows. "So we buy it and try to sell it. Then the real owner sees it. Then what?"

"Sorry," said the other. "We can't buy it. Bring us some gold instead."

I tried to hide my dismay. "Oh well, if you don't want it I'll find someone who does."

We went up and down the street, asking at every shop, but no one wanted to buy the statue.

"Come on," said Conan, "forget it. We can sell it somewhere else, where they're not so fussy. It's time we got out of this city."

But already it was too late.

"There he is!" someone shouted. "Stop thief! Catch him!"

I darted out of the shadowed alley into the bright, sunlit square. My eyes were slow to adjust to the light. I saw Theon and dodged him, only to run right into Pallas and Maximus, the gardener. Maximus, a great big bear of a man, grabbed me and held me tightly.

Theon opened the schoolbag and took out the ivory figure. "Aha! Here it is! I told you, didn't I?"

Pallas looked shocked. "Wait till the master hears about this," he said, grimly.

By now, a small crowd had gathered round us. I could see Conan on the edge of it, wondering what to do. I called out to him in our own language. "Conan! Don't try anything. Just get away!"

He looked as if he wanted to help me. But it would be useless — he couldn't possibly take on Maximus, Pallas and Theon. And if they caught him, he would be punished along with me.

"Go on — get out of here!" I shouted. "I'll follow you as soon as I can. See you in Britain!"

Theon had heard my words, but he didn't care about Conan; it was me he wanted to hurt.

"I wonder what the master will do," he said, with a gloating smile. "I expect he'll sell you. I hope you go to a cruel master, who'll beat some sense into you. That's what you need, you thieving barbarian!"

XVIII

NO HOPE

I was locked up in a storeroom until the master came home. Then he sent for me. Pallas and Theon marched me into his study.

The master looked angry. "Is it true?" he demanded. "You stole my property and tried to run away?"

"Yes," I muttered, staring at the floor. What would he do? I was sure to get a beating for this.

"Never trust a barbarian," the master said to Pallas. "The only reason I bought him was because Lucia felt sorry for him. I felt at the time that it might be an expensive mistake."

Pallas said, "It was kind of you to give him a chance, sir."

The master turned to me. He said coldly, "We gave you the chance to better yourself. You could have learned our ways and become civilised. And now you've thrown that chance away."

He paused, as if he was waiting for me to say something. But I was too proud to beg for mercy, or to make promises never to run away again. How could I promise that?

"Sell him," the master ordered Pallas. "I never keep slaves who can't be trusted."

They led me away. Theon was smiling triumphantly.

As we walked down the corridor, I saw Lucia coming towards us. She must have heard what I'd done, for she gave me a reproachful look. She probably wished she'd never asked her father to buy me.

"I'm sorry," I mumbled as she passed me. But I don't think she heard.

The following day, I found myself back at the slave market. But this time I had a notice around my neck, warning that I was a thief and a runaway. People looked me over, read the notice, and turned away.

"A thief?" said the slave standing next to me. "Bad luck. No one will want you as a household slave. You'll probably end up on a farm."

"Is that so terrible?" I asked.

"Well, it depends on the farm. The good ones are all right, if you don't mind hard work."

"What about the bad ones?" I asked.

He didn't answer. But I soon found out.

***

The farm was in the hills outside Rome. It was owned by a rich man, living in the city. We never saw him. Our real master was the overseer, Publius, who ruled the place with a rod of iron.

To guard against escapes, we were chained together in groups of four. The chains were never removed. After a few days, my ankle was red and raw where the metal rubbed against it. Every step was painful.

My hands, too, were blistered and sore from the long days in the fields. We had to hoe the weeds that grew between the endless rows of vines. We worked from sunrise to sunset, with a break at noon when the heat was at its worst. The task was so boring and monotonous that every day felt like a year.

"What happens when we reach the end of the vineyard?" I asked one day.

"We go back to the beginning," said Sergius. He laughed harshly. "What's the matter, son? Not getting bored with the job, are you?"

Sergius was in my chain gang, along with Afer and Kaeso. Sergius was all right — at least he would talk to me. But Afer, the leader, hated me because I couldn't work as fast as the others, making more work for them. Then there was Kaeso, who looked as old as my grandfather. He never spoke, except in grunts. He had been on the chain gang so long that he was more like an animal than a man.

Once, I asked the others what they had done before being sold here. Afer gave me a look that meant, "Mind your own business." Sergius said, "I was a cook, and my master thought I was trying to poison him."

"Were you really?"

He laughed that bitter laugh of his. "Maybe I should have. Then I would either be dead by now or else working somewhere decent. I used to be a good cook — one of the best."

"Why did he think you were poisoning him?" I asked.

"He was old and ill, with a bad stomach. I hope he died a painful death! As for Afer, he's here because he kept running away. Isn't that right, Afer? But this place has cured him of that."

"What about *him?*" I said, looking at Kaeso.

Sergius lowered his voice — rather pointlessly, since he was chained right next to Kaeso. "They say he killed another slave in a fight. But no one knows for sure."

Old Kaeso didn't seem to hear him. He sat staring into the distance, chewing on a hunk of bread. He looked as placid as a cow chewing the cud.

At night, or on days when the weather was bad, all the slaves were locked in a cellar. It had four narrow windows, so high up that only the sky could be seen. There was no bedding, just a stone floor, but at least it was cool after the baking heat of the fields.

Often, I lay awake among the rows of snoring men. I was exhausted, but sleep would not come. I gazed up at the few stars I could glimpse through the window, wondering if Conan could see them too. How far had he gone on his journey?

At first, I clung to the faint hope that Conan might come to my rescue. After all, I had managed to rescue him. But, as time went on, that hope slowly died. Conan wouldn't even know where I was. If he had any sense, he would be heading steadily north and westwards, each day a little closer to home. Was his leg all right? Would he ever find our village — if the Romans hadn't destroyed it?

Probably, I would never find out. I would wear away the rest of my life in this horrible place.

No! There must be some way to get out. I asked Sergius if anyone had ever escaped from the farm.

"I've been here for five years," he said, "and it's only happened once. A slave managed to break loose from his chains — I don't know how — and he ran off into the hills. Publius and his men hunted him down with dogs. When they found him, they let the dogs tear him to pieces."

Afer said, "Face it, kid — you're here for life. Like the rest of us. Only you're younger, so it will be even longer for you."

"At least it's better than the salt mines," said Sergius.

I now realised what an easy life I'd had in the household of Lucius. I would give anything to be back there, even if it meant working in the kitchen again. That would be more varied and less back-breaking than endless weeding. And the food was good; the beds were soft; the people were friendly; there were feast days now and then; you could rest occasionally.

"Get moving, boy!" I felt the bite of a whip across my back. "Don't stand there dreaming. You're here to work!"

Wearily, I took up my hoe and shuffled into line.

***

The long summer days dragged on, hot and dusty. Our gang was taken off weeding and ordered to dig trenches to water the vines. By now, my hands were growing tougher, with hard skin instead of blisters, but I had a painful abscess on my ankle, where the chain kept rubbing it. Like everyone else, I was filthy, and my skin itched with flea bites.

We were treated worse than animals. Even the oxen that pulled the cart were unyoked at night and allowed to graze in a field. We wore our chains day and night. We would never be free until death released us.

At night, I lay restless, unable to sleep as my mind went over and over things. I shouldn't have taken the statue... I should have listened to Conan... we should have left Rome at once... by now, we would be halfway across Gaul... And I thought how much I hated Theon, and what I'd do to him if I ever got the chance.

Round and round — my thoughts went endlessly round and round, like a captured bear pacing in a narrow cage. I could not spend the rest of my life here. I must get out, but how? There was no way out.

One night, I felt desperate enough to kill myself. But I didn't have a weapon to do it with. I would have to starve myself to death, or pick a fight with Kaeso, the murderer. I couldn't bear to live this life. I was weary, so weary.

All at once, I remembered something Tiro had said. Tiro, like me, could not read but was good at memorising things. He had learned by heart many of the sayings of Jesus. This was one of them: "Come to me, all you who are weary and have heavy loads to carry. I will give you rest."

Rest... that was what I longed for. But then I remembered how I had turned away from God. I'd disobeyed him. When I stole the statue, I knew I was doing wrong, but I still did it.

"Come to me, all you who are weary..."

Would he let me come to him, though? If only I had some gift to bring him, some kind of sacrifice to please him. Then he might be kind to me.

But I could still hear Tiro's voice in my memory. "Because Jesus died, we don't need to make sacrifices to please God. If we believe in Jesus, we can come near to God at any time. We can know his love, like children know the love of their father."

Was it really true?

"Please, God, hear me," I prayed. "I'm sorry I stole those things. I want to come to you. I want you to be my father. I'm so weary... Please give me rest."

A feeling of peace came over me, like my mother's hand stroking my forehead, smoothing away all my troubled thoughts. I lay back with a sigh. Very soon, I fell asleep.

***

Next day, things were back to normal, but not quite. As we ate our morning bread ration, I still felt strangely peaceful. I'd had a good night's sleep. Perhaps that was why I felt better than usual.

Publius shouted out the day's orders. "Afer's gang, carry on where you finished yesterday, down by the road."

The others groaned, for it meant a long trudge to the far boundary of the farm. But I didn't mind working near the road. The few people who might pass by were more interesting to look at than vines, vines and more vines.

Today, though, the road was almost empty. A couple of ox carts went by. Then, in the distance, I saw a cloud of dust, which meant a faster-moving vehicle, probably a rich man's carriage. As it drew closer, I saw it was pulled by four matching black horses, like Lucius' carriage horses. The coachman was black too. The coachman was –

"Tiro!" I yelled, at the top of my voice.

XIX

TOO COSTLY

As soon as he heard me, Tiro reined in the horses. Luckily, the carriage was empty — Tiro must be taking the horses out for exercise. He wouldn't have dared to stop if the master had been there.

He jumped down, hitched the horses to a tree and came running over.

"Bryn! I've been looking for you for ages!" He hugged me. He didn't seem to care about my filthy state.

"Oh, Tiro, it's great to see you!" I swallowed hard to stop my voice from shaking. "How did you find me?"

"Pallas thought you were on a farm somewhere around here — he didn't know for sure. But whenever I exercised the horses, I drove out this way, hoping and praying I'd see you. Are you all right?"

"I'm alive. Just about."

He stood back and took a proper look at me — skinny, ragged and dirty, with whip marks on my back — and his eyes filled with pity.

"Can you help me get out of here?" I whispered.

"If I can, I will."

For a moment, I imagined the entire chain gang clambering into the carriage and escaping down the road. But two of Publius' men were approaching fast.

"What's going on here?" one of them demanded.

Tiro stepped forward. "I would like to buy this slave," he said. "How much do you want for him?"

The two men looked at each other uncertainly. This had never happened before. No one ever wanted to buy slaves like us, the lowest of the low.

"You'll have to talk to Publius, the overseer. He's up at the house — just follow that track there."

Tiro thanked them and went off up the track, leaving the other slaves open-mouthed.

"Who was that, then? Your long-lost father?" Afer jeered. "I must say, you don't look very like him."

"All right, the excitement's over," we were told. "Now, get back to work."

It seemed ages before Tiro came back. When I saw his face, my heart sank. Was Publius refusing to sell me?

"Oh, he'll sell you all right," said Tiro. "But he wants 800 denarii."

"What, 800? For a kid like that?" said Afer, scornfully. "A grown man is only worth 500!"

"Didn't you bargain with him?" I said, dismayed.

"I tried, but he wouldn't go any lower. I shouldn't have let him see how much I wanted to buy you." Tiro was looking downcast. "But don't worry. I'll find the money somehow, Bryn. I'll be back soon, I promise."

I couldn't speak. Silently, I waved goodbye, and gazed after the carriage until it was just a speck in the distance.

Afer laughed. "And that's the last you'll see of him."

"No. He wouldn't lie to me," I said. "Tiro never tells lies."

But 800 denarii — that was a lot of money. Even if Tiro asked all his Christian friends to help, how could he ever find enough? I knew Tiro would do his best to help me, but his best might not be enough.

Several days went by. My heart sank lower and lower.

"What's happened to your African friend?" Afer mocked me. "He must have decided the price was too high. And he's right. You're not worth 8 denarii, never mind 800."

"Oh, leave the kid alone," said Sergius.

"Who says?"

"I do. You've been picking on him ever since he got here. Give it a rest, can't you?"

Afer glared at him. "I'm the boss of this gang. No one tells *me* what to do."

A fight broke out — an ugly, vicious fight between two men who were chained together and couldn't escape each other. They fell over, dragging me down with them. I tried to shield myself from their wild punches.

Publius' men watched the fight for a while, enjoying it. Then they stepped in with their whips. Sergius and Afer both got a savage beating. From then on, Afer hated me more than ever, as if it was all my fault.

I would have tried to keep out of his way, but that was impossible. It's frightening to spend your entire life, waking and sleeping, right next to someone who loathes you. Once again, I was having trouble getting to sleep — I was scared that Afer might kill me in the night.

My prayers now were angry ones: "Can't you hear me? You're supposed to love me like a father. What father would let his son be treated like this?"

But no answer came.

***

The burning heat of summer began to cool slightly. Grapes were ripening on the vines. Sergius warned me that we would have to work even harder than usual at harvest time. "Then, when the grapes and olives are harvested, we get a bit of a rest."

Yes, and after that the whole thing would start all over again. Weeding... digging... watering... harvesting... on and on, year after year of it, until I became a worn-out, empty shell, like old Kaeso.

I thought I'd given up hoping. But whenever we were near the road, I couldn't stop myself looking out for Tiro. Every time a carriage came into sight, I watched eagerly until it was close enough to destroy my hopes yet again.

Then one evening, as we made our way wearily back from the fields, I stopped suddenly. I couldn't believe my eyes. There, outside the house, was the carriage with its four black horses.

The door of the house opened, and Tiro came out with Publius. I hardly dared to look at Tiro's face — but when I did, I saw he was smiling.

Publius called to one of his men. "Take Afer's gang to the blacksmith. Tell him to unshackle the boy there. He's been sold."

The blacksmith worked in a shed near the stables. Using a hammer and chisel, he struck off the metal collar which had chafed my ankle for so long. I enjoyed the look of hatred and envy on Afer's face. But Sergius had been a friend to me — I was sorry I couldn't rescue him from the farm.

"Goodbye," I said to him. "I hope you get out of here one day."

Then I hurried back to Tiro. I would have run and jumped for joy, but my legs weren't used to freedom yet. My right ankle still seemed to feel the weight of the chain.

Tiro said polite farewells to Publius. Then he helped me up to sit beside him on the driver's bench of the carriage. "Let's get out of this place," he muttered, taking up the reins.

He took things slowly on the rutted track that led down to the main road. He didn't want to damage the wheels of the carriage. Before we were halfway down the hill, a great commotion broke out behind us — voices shouting, dogs barking. I craned my neck to look back, feeling suddenly frightened. They couldn't stop me now — could they?

"Don't worry," said Tiro. "You've been bought and paid for. You don't belong there any more."

I grabbed Tiro's arm. "There's someone following us," I whispered. "Look — over there."

Tiro saw it too, a shadowy figure slipping between the rows of vines. He flicked the reins to make the horses speed up. But as they gathered pace, someone dashed out of the vineyard, grabbed on to the rear of the carriage and swung himself up.

I gasped. It was Sergius.

"Don't stop," he said breathlessly, crouching down on the floor. "Drive on — please."

After one glance at him, Tiro obeyed. We swung onto the main road and headed towards Rome at a good, fast pace. Sergius began to laugh.

"They won't catch me, even if they set a hundred dogs on my trail. Ha! I wish I could see Publius' face right now!"

"What happened?" I demanded. "How did you escape?"

"The guard got careless. He was talking to the blacksmith, instead of watching us. Afer got behind him, and whacked him with a hammer. Kaeso took out the blacksmith — knocked him out cold. Easy as anything! We knew we hadn't much time, so we freed each other and then ran off in different directions. I don't suppose old Kaeso will get far, though."

I hoped he was wrong. I even hoped Afer would get away. No one, however mean, deserved the sort of life we had been forced to live.

"Where do you want us to take you?" Tiro asked.

"Just drop me off in the outskirts of Rome. Anywhere that's good and crowded."

It was getting dark by the time we reached Rome. In a crowded neighbourhood where many poor people lived, Sergius thanked us and said goodbye. Then he disappeared down a narrow side street. I don't know what happened to him — I never saw him again.

XX

CHOICES

Tiro had arranged for me to stay with Crispus and Marcella. He dropped me off near their house.

"I have to go," he said. "I'll be in trouble if the master suddenly decides he needs the carriage."

He drove off. I realised he'd taken quite a risk for my sake. And I hadn't even thanked him properly. I wanted to run after him. But I couldn't follow him to Lucius' house. It would only cause more trouble — the master would want to know why Tiro was still friendly with a thief like me.

Never mind; I could talk to him the next time he came to visit Crispus and Marcella. I found my way to their house, where they gave me a warm welcome. After having a good meal, a wash and a change of clothes, I felt almost my old self again.

Apparently, I didn't look like my old self, though. "You're so thin," said Marcella. "We must feed you up.

And you've grown taller, and lost that pale northern look you used to have." This was true. The baking heat of the vineyard had tanned my skin as brown as a Roman's.

"Do you still plan on returning to Britain?" Crispus asked.

I nodded. I had talked about this with Tiro on the drive back to Rome. Officially, I was his slave, since he had paid for me. But Tiro had laughed at this idea. "What would I want a slave for? I bought you so as to set you free. And I know you've always wanted to go home."

My heart leaped. At once, I started thinking about the journey, making plans.

But now, Marcella was trying to persuade me not to go — or at least, not yet. "Winter will soon be here, and no one travels in winter if they can help it. You should stay in Rome for a few months. Start your journey in the spring, when you're fit and well again."

"I want to catch up with my brother," I said, although I knew it was unlikely. Conan had left months ago. Where would he be when winter came? Perhaps he would be stuck in the mountains somewhere, or stranded on this side of the sea crossing. Perhaps, if he was very lucky, he would manage to get home.

But what if he reached the place where our village used to be, only to find the Romans had destroyed it? No home, no family, nothing to live on and winter approaching... I shivered.

Maybe I should stay in Rome for the winter, as Marcella said. I would have to find work of some kind so that I could pay for my food. I couldn't live on her kindness all winter.

A few days later, Tiro called round. I thanked him for everything he'd done. Then I asked him a question which had been bothering me. "Tiro, where did you get the money to pay Publius? Was it from the Christians?"

"Some of it was."

"Not all? What about the rest?"

He hesitated, then said, "The rest was mine."

"Do you mean the money you've been saving up to buy your own freedom?"

"Yes."

"And how much have you got left?"

"Nothing," he said, quietly.

I stared at him. It was an incredible gift. I knew he'd been saving up that money for years — now he would have to start all over again. For my sake, he would have to serve many more years as a slave. He might be an old man before he could be free.

"Oh, Tiro..." There were no words to thank him enough. For I could see by his face that the choice hadn't been an easy one.

I couldn't think of anyone else who would give up so much for me — not even my own brother. Perhaps my father would have loved me enough to do it... perhaps not.

"Tiro, you are better than a father to me," I said.

He put his arm around me. "And you are like my son... like the son that I lost long ago. In years to come, I'll think of you. My two sons, one in the distant south

— if he's still alive — and one far away to the north."
He smiled, but his dark eyes were full of sadness.

The next day, I spent a long time thinking. For more than a year I had been longing to go home. A thousand times over, I'd imagined returning to our village and meeting my family again.

But maybe none of them existed any more, except in my memories. Even those memories were growing fainter. I found it hard to picture my sisters' faces or remember my mother's voice. Did that mean they were dead? There was no way of finding out without making the long journey home. And that would mean saying goodbye to Tiro.

I felt as if I was being dragged in two directions, like a bone between two dogs. Tiro had given up so much for me. How could I simply leave, disappear from his life, as if I didn't care what happened to him?

I talked to Crispus and Marcella, who were amazed to hear what Tiro had done. He had kept it secret even from his friends.

Crispus said, "He gave up his own chance of freedom so that you could be free?"

"He was following the Master," said Marcella. "He was being like Jesus, who gave up his life for us."

"Yes," said Crispus. "'Love each other as I have loved you.' That's what Jesus tells us to do."

I said, "I don't know how I can ever repay Tiro. I can find work and give him the money I earn, but that won't be very much. He still won't be free for ages."

I was sure Tiro didn't expect me to repay him. He had set me free as a gift, asking nothing in return. I could leave Rome for ever, and he wouldn't try to stop me. And yet...

This was hard. I was so used to being ordered about, told what to do and where to go. But now I was free, and I had to make my own choices.

Free — yet not free. I remembered my prayer that night in prison, when I asked God to be my father. A son should obey his father. What would God want me to do?

"Love each other as I have loved you..."

All at once, I made up my mind. I would stay in Rome, find work, and help Tiro save up the price of his freedom. Then he would know that my gratitude was more than empty words.

Maybe one day I could go home. I couldn't give up the thought of it entirely — but for now my place was in Rome.

***

Crispus and Marcella thought my decision was a good one. They told me I could stay with them for as long as I liked.

I asked Crispus what sort of work I might be able to do, explaining that I'd spent some time working in a rich man's kitchen. He looked thoughtful.

"How much do you know about baking bread?"

"I don't know what goes into it — the cook did all that. But I can knead the dough and shape it all right."

He said, "We could use an assistant in our bakery. My niece used to help out, but she's just got married. Would you be interested? We can't pay very much..."

"And it's hard work at busy times," put in Marcella.

I grinned to myself. She didn't know what hard work meant. This job would be easy compared to life on the farm.

"Think about it," said Crispus. "You don't need to decide right away."

Another choice to make! Next day, I asked Tiro what he thought. It was the evening when the Christians met together, but Tiro had arrived early.

At first, he didn't understand me rightly. "Work for Crispus and Marcella? You mean, you're planning to stay in Rome for the winter? That's good," he said.

"Not just for the winter. I'm going to stay for a long time — until you're free, Tiro."

"That's even better." His smile seemed to light up the room.

"And everything I earn is yours — I owe you that."

Tiro began to argue, as I knew he would. So I changed the subject. "You haven't answered my question. What do you think Crispus would be like as a boss?" As I said it, Crispus walked into the room.

"Oh, he'd be terrible," said Tiro, grinning at his friend. "Even worse than Quintus. He'll make you work night and day, and beat you if you complain."

"If he does, I can always leave," I said. It was an odd feeling. I wasn't a slave any more. I didn't have to go on doing work I hated — I could simply walk away from it. Rome was a big place. There would be other jobs I could do.

When I first came to Rome, I hated and feared it. I thought all Romans were my enemies. But now I was used to the place, and I knew that the Romans, just like my own tribe, were a mixture of good and bad, kindness and cruelty. The city, too, was a mixture, with all its wealth, poverty, grand temples and crowded slums.

I couldn't say I belonged there, or felt at home. But I did have friends, and of course I had Tiro, who was almost like family. And I had God as my father — the one true God, the Lord of all the earth. If I hadn't come to Rome, I would never have known him.

Looking back, I saw how much the past year had changed me. I was no longer a frightened child, a captive surrounded by strangers who spoke an unknown language. I'd grown up a lot. I was almost a man, able to earn my own living and make my own choices.

And best of all — I was free. My year of slavery was over.

Rome in flames

What will happen next? Bryn's adventures
continue…

"How did the fire begin? No one
seemed to know. Some people believed
it was started deliberately. Others said it
was an accident, when a cook dropped
a pan of oil, or a child was careless with
a candle. It wouldn't be the first time.
During the hot summer months,
outbreaks of fire were quite common in
the city.

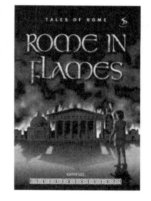

But this was no ordinary fire. This was
the great fire of Rome."

The Christians are having to meet in secret as the emperor's
hatred for them grows. And Bryn is still facing danger at every
turn; fighting the flames, escaping the city and returning to even
more danger…

(Published October 2005)

ISBN 1 84427 089 0

**You can buy these books at your local Christian bookshop,
or online at www.scriptureunion.org.uk/publishing
or call Mail Order direct: 08450 706 006**